BLOOD O1

GROUND

and other short stories

Michael Wombat

Copyright © 2014 Michael Wombat

Cover design by Thom White (thomwhite.co.uk)

ISBN: 978-1-291-95830-0

CONTENTS

PREAMBLE

Welcome, beloved reader, to this eclectic melange of outpourings from the Wombat brain.

Eclectic (adj): deriving ideas, style, or taste from a broad and diverse range of sources.

You will understand, therefore, that there is no underlying theme to these gobbets of whimsy, save that I wrote them, often while in my cups. I hope to amuse, entertain, thrill and frighten you. Most of all, I hope to surprise you. You should expect the unexpected, including (sadly) the occasional cliché just like that one. You may have read one or two of these stories in other places, but there is plenty of hitherto unpublished material here, too.

As ever, the genius that is Thom White has my undying gratitude for the superb cover design, as well as my continuing respect and admiration simply for being such a fine chap. The universe needs more fine chaps such as he.

Right, that's enough jaw flapping. Read on, pilgrim.

BLOOD ON THE

GROUND

Blood on the Ground, *my first foray into the Western genre, was inspired by my accidental discovery of the Rex Wells version of the Tex Ritter song 'Blood on the Saddle'. The story subsequently appeared in the Anthology Club collection, 'Soul of the Universe' (available on Amazon). Other influences on the tale include the film 'Jeremiah Johnson' and, although you might not immediately see it, Joss Whedon's 'Firefly'. My thanks to @tc_cornesto for Rence's name.*

The rise is a swathe of white, broken only by the occasional smudge of stone and a swirl of grey mist. From this angle a slant of hazy sun scatters a sparkle across the wide stretch of snow. A powder blue southern sky ends abruptly at a rapidly advancing and toweringly dark cloud formation.

Rence narrows his eyes and squints back the way they've come. The marks of their passing are quickly disappearing under a drifting mist of fine snow. The faint hazed procession of trees way back down the hill runs unbroken and uninterrupted across the arc of his vision.

"I think we lost the tracker, Red, don't you? I can't see a damn thing moving down there. Maybe we're home free, huh?"

Silence. Rence pulls his *"Boss of the Plains"* hat down further to his freezing ears, and tightens the muffler about his mouth to stop his breath from freezing. His moustache bristles with ice.

"Aw hell, Red," Rence mutters, "This don't make no sense. How in hell did we end up here anyway? It was only a god-damned stick."

Red does not answer him. Normally Red's silence does not surprise Rence because Red is a horse. This time, however, the silence does not surprise Rence because Red is dead.

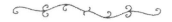

The happy trail that led to this God-abandoned wasteland of cold had started, ironically, in a smoke-filled saloon that was as hot as a whorehouse on nickel night.

"Gimme another shot of that oh-be-joyful, Zedock," Rence yelled to the bartender, flinging a coin across to him. Cheap whiskey sloshed into his glass.

Rence nursed his glass, sipping only occasionally, and listened to the babbling crowd of customers. A painted lady of the line, easily fifty years old, sang tunelessly along to a clanking piano; a song about a puddle of blood and a saddle splattered with gore. It suited the rank atmosphere of the run-down bar perfectly.

Rence's bankroll was running low and he was on the lookout for some easy tin. Men were loose-lipped when they were soaked, and a full saloon was a good place to pick up information that might lead to easy enrichment. Take the two gumps behind Rence, for example.

"She a looker?" asked the first.

"Nah, she looks like she's been rode hard and put up wet, but I tell you she's sitting on an almighty heap of gold up at Powder Bluff."

"Then why don't nobody go just take it?"

"Some have tried, sure, but they all bar one ended up buzzard food. There's something mighty dangerous about that tribe, if you ask me."

"I thought Crow were friendly?"

"Mostly, that's the case, but not Pine Leaf's crew. Folk say a body had best steer well clear of that camp, no matter the temptation."

"What folk?"

"Slitnose Jonah, for one. He went up there last week and came back scareder than a chicken in a high wind. Hair turned white, spouting nonsense, pissing hisself."

"Hellfire."

"Yup, I seen him myself. It was a shaker, a solid shaker. So shut your big bazoo and get me another drink."

Rence had heard enough. Pay dirt. He need pay no mind to the story of Slitnose Jonah's terror. That tale was obviously fiddle-faddle, put out to keep cheap bandits away. Rence was a step above, made of sterner stuff than most, and he was as good a thief as they come. He'd pull this one off.

He downed his whiskey and left the saloon, relieved to feel fresh air on his skin after the sordid reek of the saloon. Red snorted as he approached and nuzzled affectionately at Rence's hand. The man stroked the horse's nose.

"Not yet, pard," Rence told him. "We'll eat after the job's done. Come on. Let's steal some gold."

He climbed into the saddle and rode west out of town. Riding at night did not worry him as it did some. It was easier to hide at night, for starters, and a man with sharp eyes could see just as well as in daylight, as long as there was at least a sliver of moon up there in the black. Tonight the moon was full, baring her whole self to the world like a cheap wanton.

Not that there was a right lot to see. They rode a while through a scrubby wasteland of nothing before rounding to the north and moving into the foothills of the craggy mountain that soared above the valley.

A short spell later, up near Powder Bluff, he could make out a scattering of five or six tipis ahead. They were arranged in a rough circle, their pointed tips silhouetted against a mooncast sky. Rence dismounted and removed his gunbelt so as not to rattle and the easier to crouch, and stowed them temporarily in the travel bag that hung from Red's saddle.

He left the horse to wait behind a rock shaped like a wolf's head. Red knew to stay quiet and to wait for Rence's return, as he had done many times previous.

Rence crept toward the tipis, keeping low, a capacious saddle-bag slung on his back to carry whatever goodies he might find. A great fire barked and crackled at the centre of the camp. Crow men and women warmed themselves around it, some sitting and talking, others meandering about, drinking and smoking. A few men were playing a game involving sticks, a rough ball and much shouting. Several large dogs lay gnawing at bone or hide, or chased shadows around the camp.

The women wore dresses decorated with complex beadwork and accessories of what looked like animal teeth. They wore their hair in two braids, interwoven with crow feathers. The men wore shirts, leggings and a long breechcloth, similarly beaded. Without exception their hair was long, though a few wore two hair pipes made from beads on either side of their head. One proud brave had what appeared to be a stuffed crow on his head.

Their merry shadows fluttered dark across the tipis, which were also intricately decorated. Big on beads, were the Crow.

Rence figured that he'd come at a good time, when all the tribe were outside enjoying a rip-roaring party. There was a more than good chance that he would be able investigate the tipis uninterrupted. He snaked towards the nearest and peered quickly beneath the flap. It was empty, and he slipped inside.

Any sizeable amount of dinero would likely be kept in sacks, or chests, or some other large container. He did not think that it could be buried, for the ground here on the bluff was rocky and hard to dig. No, what he was looking for was storage big enough to hold a fortune. He circled the inside of the tipi, but found nothing interesting among the ordinary clutter of hides, pots and a pile of half-fletched arrows. There was a wolf-pelt, which might have brought some value, but it was awful cumbersome. Rence had heard that the Crow often used a wolf-pelt disguise when they were hunting bison on foot. He thought that was stupid, and that they'd be better off using horses and guns.

The next tipi was the same: a right lot of clutter but little of value. He did pick up a beautifully decorated stick, some three feet long, it was decorated with odd carvings, notches and feathers, with an eagle claw fixed to one end. He figured that he'd likely manage to sell it for a pretty price to some unsalted dude visiting from the East, and slipped it into his bag, tying a beaded decoration to the bag-strap so that the stick would not fall out.

He was readying to move on to the next tipi when he heard loud female laughter from outside. He threw himself into a dark corner, hastily pulling up a blanket to cover himself and hauling his boots under it.

Four laughing Crow women ducked into the tipi, yammering away nineteen to the dozen. The woman at the rear, a little older than the rest and ugly as a mud fence, said something in Crow that caused her companions to burst into wild laughter. She reached down and caressed the buttocks of the young girl nearest to her, who smiled.

God damn.

The girl turned and pulled old Plain Jane to her, moulding their two bodies together, swaying. Rence had never seen the like. He had heard of such fancy goings on back East, but had imagined that they were confined to whores and French women. This was...

God damn.

The two other women approached the pair and stooped to lift Plain Jane's dress over her head. She swayed naked in the dim light.

Rence stifled a gasp. Although her face looked like the hindquarters of bad luck, her body was something else. He stared for a spell while kissing and, well, other things went on. Then, as much as he wanted to stay and watch the other women get unshucked too, he got set to make tracks. He was not such a fool as to ignore such an ideal opportunity to leave undetected.

He edged quietly towards the entrance, silent as a bone orchard. Silent, that is, until the purloined stick poking out of his bag clattered against a large pot.

"*Iaxassee bacheé!*" screamed one of the women. Rence leapt to his feet and legged it out of the tipi full chisel. He sprinted lickety-split towards the wolf's head rock. Screams and yells rent the air behind him. A swift arrow whipped close by his ear, and a dog snapped at his heels as he vaulted astride Red's ready back and spurred the horse into action. They rode like Sam Hill himself was after them, away from the hollering camp.

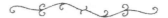

Snow flurries dance and whirl as the fall increases and the wind kicks up. Rence's ears are turning numb, and he tries to pull his muffler higher to cover them. That proves to be surprisingly difficult when you're lying on your side. How the hell long has he been here now? Seems like hours. He begins to shiver uncontrollably and his belly complains once more that it needs food.

He is in a peck of trouble. He'll be ended if he stays here. He has to move. He folds his right leg up against his belly and plants his foot firmly against the saddle on Red's back. A deep breath, then Rence channels all his strength into pushing down on that foot, while trying to wriggle his left leg out from beneath Red's body. Fists clenched, face screwed up, he releases a scream of frustration as he moves not one inch.

He is still trapped, cold and hungry, and like to die here unless he can invent a way out. Perhaps he could dig below his trapped leg; he might gain enough space that way to drag himself free.

He reaches down and digs into the snow about his leg as far down as he can reach. The trouble is that at this spot the layer of snow is thin, and he does not manage to shift much before hitting the ice layer below. A further attempt to extract his leg fails as thoroughly as did the first.

In his saddle bag sits the perfect tool to chip away at the ice, but the bag is frustratingly out of his reach. He reaches around behind his buttocks, behind the saddle, and pulls his trail blanket from its bindings. He unrolls it quickly and wraps it about him as best he can. It helps, a little.

Wait, what is that?

Rence blinks. He holds his breath so that it won't mist his sight. There, on the grey fogged horizon, a smudge of black.

"Damn, Red. It ain't possible," he says, teeth chattering. "Must be a bird. Maybe a hare. Ain't nothing can track this high. Ain't nothing as'd want to."

Rence pushed Red on with his heels, though the horse didn't need the urging. He galloped and leapt with mighty vigour. Rence took them around the edge of Powder Bluff itself and up, knowing the qualities of his mount, and the speed that Red could make travelling uphill. More than once had this ability of Red's gotten them both out of the sticky.

Red's powerful legs pounded like pistons, his hooves thumping a staccato rhythm as the pair high-tailed through the moonlight. Red could leave most horses standing in an uphill race, even Indian paints. They would soon be out of reach of any pursuit.

Besides, the Crow were hardly likely to follow him far. He had not taken their treasure, after all, hadn't even sniffed it. That job had come a cropper damn fast. He had barely started looking before having to take his leave.

He glanced backward. The whole tribe seemed to be shouting at him from the foot of the slope some fifty yards back, while a half dozen others urged their horses up the hill in pursuit, accompanied by a couple of dogs.

Hoo-ee, they had got their dander up alright. Maybe that was because he'd seen Miss Fancy Pants in the buck or something. Maybe she was a high-up in the tribe. Chief, even. Rence knew that Crow women were respected by the tribe, and were able to rise high, even to chief if they possessed the will.

He risked another glance back. Most of the pursuers had given up, a lone rider now chasing him. He turned Red around a big boulder. The horse stumbled over a crevice for one heart-stopping moment, but managed to right himself and carry on. Rence spurred him higher.

Now there was a beef-headed idea, if you asked Rence. Women in charge? Women don't got no place bossing men about. That would never happen in civilised society as long as Rence had a hole in his ass.

Mind, Miss Fancy Pants might have had a face like a cow's leavings, but from the neck down she had been a sight to see. Rence's mind drifted on this, and he allowed Red to slow his pace, eventually coming to a stop by a stand of scraggy bushes.

He looked back down the moonswept slope. All good and daisy. No-one was behind him now. He grinned and reached into his yannigan bag for something to chew on, but grasped at air.

What in tarnation?

He stared once again down the slope, this time taking in a small bundle down by the big boulder they had passed just a few minutes ago. His bag. It must have fallen from the saddle when Red stumbled. Hell, he needed that bag. It contained everything he owned - an extra set of clothes, extra ammunition, food, a few useful pieces of equipment, playing cards, a bill of sale for his Red, his harmonica: his whole life, in fact. Damn; his handgun was in there too.

As he watched, a lone rider rounded the big boulder, moving slow. The rider paused by Rence's bag, dismounted and rifled through the pack before throwing it down, scattering Rence's belongings on the ground.

The rider remounted and carried on towards Rence. Idiot, why'd he want to do that? Why didn't he just turn about? There weren't no profit in dogging Rence now.

Rence took up the reins again and clicked his tongue, urging Red onward through the scrub. He had no need to gallop now. A gentle trot from Red would still outpace the tired Crow pursuer. He still hoped that the man would give up the chase soon. He had no desire to waste bullets on the Injun if he didn't have to. Bullets cost money.

A long rise, rock and scrub-strewn, stretched out before him. Perhaps a mile ahead was a line of dark trees, and beyond those the land shone white under the moon. It was snowy up there. Rence had tried hunting up beyond the snowline once but it had been damned hard work. Stealing was much easier, and more rewarding. He figured that if he moseyed on up there now, though, the cold would likely cause the Crow to fall off his trail and turn back.

Strange persons, them Injuns. They had some mighty funny ideas, like for example sometimes letting women be chief. Rence had also heard tell of the *koskalaka;* men who dressed and lived as women, or women who lived as men. Two-spirited, the Injuns called them, and paid them respect. Weirdoes, Rence called them. Crazy as corn on a hot stove.

A couple of hours hour later, as dawn lifted the sky, he entered the trees. Red plodded dutifully on despite his growing tiredness after negotiating the rough surface of the hill by moonlight.

Higher still they climbed, at a slow pace but steady, weaving the dark spaces between the soaring trunks. A further hour and a half saw them emerge onto a snow-covered slope in full daylight. There was a break in the trees here of maybe half a mile, a gentle white slope stretching up between him and another stand of trees sitting to the left. Past that the mountain continued to rise slowly for a while until the rock slammed up in a vertical crag.

Red huffed out big clouded breaths, and snorted. The air was thin this high, and it was coming on chill.

"I'm banded too, Red, but we have to deal with this afore we eat," Rence told the horse. "Won't take but a short ride to get back down to grass once we're a-right. Don't fret."

There weren't no point in checking behind him now. All he'd see would be trees. Better to get some space behind him first. Find a sitting spot up by that stand, maybe, and wait to see whether the Injun poked his nose out to be shot at.

He walked Red onward and upward, slowly now. The horse's hooves disturbed shallow fallen snow which gradually grew deeper the higher they climbed.

His belly rumbled. Damn, he was wolfishly peckish. Maybe after he'd gotten rid of the Injun he'd be able to shoot himself a rabbit, or even a buck. Rence was no hunter, he lacked the patience, but he was a fair shot and needs must when the devil drives.

The sun glittered on the snow, a myriad diamonds sprinkled beneath their feet. It was beautiful up here. He'd maybe spend time above the snowline another day, when he wasn't being nagged by Injuns, hunger and thirst. He reached for his canteen. Blast! Why in hell had he put it in his bag last night? The mere absence of water made his throat feel drier.

A light snow began to drift down, probably from those storm-tall clouds moving in from the north. He opened his lips and faced the sky, allowing a few cold flakes to glide onto his tongue. They only served to heighten his thirst. The temptation to dismount and scoop up a handful of snow was huge, but he figured he'd be better waiting until he found some cover.

And that cover looked to be just ahead. A couple of hundred yards short of the small stand of trees lay an old cedar, long time fallen. That would make good hiding; he had almost missed it his own self, snow-coated as it was. Rence steered Red to the far side and dismounted. He knelt and scooped a handful of snow from the wide trunk. Sweet relief flooded through him as he touched it to his tongue. He held a palmful for Red to lap up.

Rence drew his .50 Hawken rifle from its saddle holster. He'd stolen the gun from a drunk hunter who'd been passing through town on his way Fort Lupus trading post. It was a right smart shooting iron.

He took a paper cartridge from the saddle pouch and bit off the end. He poured the powder into the barrel, then stuffed in the ball encased in the paper wrapping. He ram-rodded the projectile home and primed the pan.

Laying the Hawken ready on the trunk of the fallen tree, he took Red's bridle.

"Go low, Red," he said, stroking the horse's nose, "You need to be invisible too."

Red obediently bent his legs and lay on his side, snorting his displeasure. He was an obedient horse, though, and would stay low until told to stand. Rence sat behind the trunk and laid the Hawken across his lap. His backside was cold, but he was ready.

He peered down the hill, seeing no movement by the trees that they'd left a short time ago. Good. He'd give it half an hour and if nothing appeared then it was a good assume that the chase had been abandoned.

While he waited he punished the air with his singing, keeping his voice low, crooning the little tune that he'd not been able to get out of his head since the previous evening.

As he sang softly of the slaughtered cowboy whose blood was soaking the ground, Rence keenly examined the far horizon and the sky.

Those clouds were moving in from the north. Like to be overhead soon. For now though, the sun still shone weakly and the sky to the south kept blue. There was nothing to see, not even a rabbit or a bird, though he heard the *KEEEE* of an eagle. His thoughts of shooting a meal for himself now seemed... damn, what was that?

A rider emerged from the distant trees and halted. The figure looked at the ground, his small horse standing patiently, then raised his eyes in Rence's direction. Rence held his breath, though that hardly mattered at this distance. He pulled the rear trigger of his rifle, thereby setting the front trigger ready to fire on a light touch. There was no point in loosing a bullet yet – the figure was some five hundred yards away, well out of the Hawken's range – but it hurt nothing to be ready.

The distant figure must have been satisfied that the coast was clear, because he commenced once more to ride up the slope, dogging Rence's earlier tracks. Stupid, stupid Injun. Just give it up already.

The fallen tree would be about invisible from down there.

"Come on, shitbreeches," Rence muttered impatiently, "When I'm done with you, there won't be enough of you left to snore."

Four hundred yards now, just about within range, but Rence waited still, eyes narrowed against the white glare, wanting to be certain of this shot. Three hundred and fifty yards and still he waited. Three hundred yards and Rence gently caressed the front trigger of the Hawken.

A deafening report echoed from the trees and the mountain behind him. A cloud of smoke plumed upward from his gun, and he saw his pursuer's head snap back as the bullet hit, blood or maybe brains splashing out of the skull. The figure collapsed backwards off his pony.

"Yeehaw!" yelled Rence, "Gotcha, you son of a whore!" He leapt to his feet and gazed down the slope. The figure lay still on the ground, his horse standing idly nearby. Rence turned and got Red to his feet. He would ride back down and claim his prize – a pony and who knew what else – and then find food. His belly gurgled at the thought.

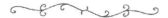

The smudge is growing perceptibly larger, but it is hard to make out an actual shape through the increasing snow. It is just a blotch, a blur of a somewhat darker grey than its surroundings, nothing more. Could maybe be a passing deer. Or if he's lucky, could be the fur-trapper returning.

The thought of deer drags his mind back to his belly. It feels like days since he ate, although he knows it must be no more than twenty-four hours. What he wouldn't give now for that pemmican in his lost yannigan bag. He smirks at the juxtaposition of words. Pemmican in the yannigan, heh. His smirk quickly turns into a despairing moan, however, as his hunger bites.

A trickle of red slices through the pure white just inches from his head. The blue is all gone from the sky: there remain only shades of white, and grey. The whole world is monochrome but for this slash of red — a crimson liquid flowing down the slope near his head.

Blood on the ground.

The blood run freezes at the extremities of its reach, but enough keeps pulsing from behind to push the flow further into his vision.

He reaches out a gloved hand and scoops the scarlet snow to his mouth, giving him for the briefest moment an illusion of sustenance. The bloody snow tastes of wet metal and frozen earth.

His left leg is numb now, can't hardly sense it. He feels a little drowsy, and wishes the trapper would hurry.

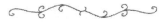

Rence patted Red's neck, satisfied, and got him to his feet.

"Whatcha shootin' at, wanderer?"

The rough voice came from behind. He turned to see a fat old man rolling down the hill leading a skinny old piebald. Although on closer inspection, maybe the man wasn't fat at all. Maybe his rotundity was due to the copious number of furs that swathed his body — mostly beaver pelts, but some rabbit and other furs and hides that Rence could not identify. The man sported a huge black beard, and his head was crowned by an impressive beaver fur hat, the flat spade of a tail still attached and hanging down between his shoulders. His horse too was bedizened with furs.

"Th'art a mite underdressed to be this high, traveller," the man told him as he approached. "Lost your way?"

"Nope," Rence answered, "Day trip only. Heading back down to warm civilisation quicker than quick."

"Civilisation's still down there, is it? Bah, then I'll come no lower, thank 'ee very much. Don't hold much love for civilisation. Too crowded, too dirty, too noisy, too persnickity. Name's Jebediah Smith, at your service. Got a pole lodge in the trees over there, should you need a rest before descending."

"Terence Corness. Think I'll be fine, thanks."

"As you want. I am genuinely pleased to happen across you, Terence Corness. It's been too many days since I last heard human speech."

"Then I regret that the first you heard was my sorry excuse for a voice. You hunting beaver, Jebediah? You look well loaded up with fur."

"Been trapping for these last months. Heading over to Fort Lupus now for the rendezvous. Lotsa unwelcome hoopla and rambunctiousness at a rendezvous, but I got to sell me these furs." The trapper's eyes narrowed. "Heard you shoot, day tripper. Rabbit was it? Be mostly rabbit round here. No elk this time of year."

Rence remained silent. Smith rummaged among his furs and drew out an eyeglass, a small telescope that glinted as he lifted it to his eye and scanned the slope below.

"Huh!" he grunted, "So, you hunt bigger prey than rabbit. What's the story here, day tripper?"

"That there's an Injun been trailing me for a time now. I figured he meant to do me harm, so I did him harm first. Killed him first shot."

"Crow, like as not. They are with no doubt the finest trackers in these parts. Dangerous, too, if'n you rile 'em. What did you do to rile this 'un?"

"Sweet nothing. Well, I took his stick, I suppose, but hey, it's only a stick." Rence drew the prettily designed rod from his saddle bag to show the trapper, who frowned.

"Coup stick," he said. "You took his coup stick. You know what that is?" Rence shook his head.

"Crow warriors win regard in battle by acts of dumb bravery. Any blow against an enemy counts as a coup, but the most celebrated acts include touching an enemy warrior with the hand, the bow, or," Smith brandished the stick, "with a coup stick. If they can do this without getting hurt, they win even greater respect. Coups are recorded by putting notches in a coup stick. This here is a record of one warrior's bravery. And a mighty impressive record it is at that – see all these notches?"

Rence nodded. Smith looked again down the slope through his eyeglass.

"Yep, that's a Crow pony down there. If I were you, day tripper, I'd let go the coup stick. It can only bring you trouble."

"Not any more it can't. I killed him. Saw the insides of his head."

"Well, day tripper, I ain't no doctor, so don't take this as gospel, but that Crow ain't dead. That Crow ain't a 'him' neither. That Crow's a 'her'."

"What?" Rence looked again down the slope. Sure enough, a figure was riding slowly up towards them. "The hell? There must have been two of 'em."

"On the one horse?" Smith shook his head. "More likely you just grazed her."

"I hit the head! I saw the head break apart! And what, you're telling me that's a squaw?"

"That I am. And I'll thank you not to use that word, day tripper. That's a hellfire insult, and I do count some Crow as friends."

Smith once more squinted through his eyeglass at the approaching figure, then replaced the telescope in amongst his furs.

"You don't believe I shot him," Rence said.

"Au contraire, day tripper, I do believe it. I also believe that you have a power more trouble than you can ever hope to handle. You listen to me, and listen with all your ears, cos once I finish speaking I ain't hanging around.

"I recognise this woman. Her name's Pine Leaf. She's a Crow chief and she counts coup. She counts beaucoup coup. And you're looking like to be her next notch."

"Wait, a chief? I—"

"Still your voice!" Smith snapped, glancing down the slope. "I ain't giving you much more time and you need to hear this! Pine Leaf was taken prisoner by the Crow when she was ten years old, and she's growed up in their tribe. Soon after she was taken she vowed to kill a hundred enemies by her own hand. You can see how close she is to that ambition by her stick here.

"Now, while she always wears womanly clothes, she's disposed to manly pursuits - horse keeping, hunting and warfare, mostly against the Blackfoot. She has at least four female wives, and she has a strong voice in the tribe. The Crow say she's two-spirited, *koskalaka*. You know this word?"

Rence nodded.

"Above all that and most of all, day tripper, she's a fearsome warrior... and likely more than that. Some say she's eternal. She's immortal. Some say she's... hell, she's getting too close for me. I ain't hanging around to find out what else she is."

Smith grabbed the reins of his piebald and moved quickly aslant the slope, heading east. He yelled back over his shoulder as he disappeared.

"Leave the coup stick! Your life ain't worth it!"

"Wait! You got any food?"

"In the pole lodge! You're on your own, day tripper!"

Rence was shaken by the fur trapper's clear panic and fear, but not so much that he didn't recognise horse-shit when he heard it. What complete poppycock. Immortal, my freezing ass. There was no way Rence Corness would ever be beat by a woman, and he'd damn well prove it. He took another cartridge and reloaded the Hawken.

He felt no need to hide this time, and raised the rifle to his shoulder. The blade sight lined up perfectly with the woman's midriff. She was only about a hundred yards away now, so he didn't bother to set the gun, but simply pulled the trigger hard.

The bullet hit her smack in the chest. Blood spurted from the wound as she somersaulted from the horse's back to sprawl in the snow.

Rence did not hang around, immediately sliding the Hawken back into its holster by the saddle. He swung onto Red's back and urged him up the slope, ignoring the nearby trees and Smith's pole lodge. Adrenalin overcame hunger for the moment. He'd have time later to eat, and at least now he knew where he could find food nearby.

The way ahead now was a gentler incline than before. Red made good speed. Rence untied his muffler from the pommel and wrapped it about his neck.

Eternal? Immortal? He shivered, and not just because it was getting colder.

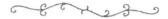

The steely grey sky grows darker. The snowfall gains in strength, big fluffy flakes now that drift across the washed-out grey world, confusing his sight.

Everything he sees is unclear, distorted. There's too much white everywhere. Too much grey. Too much... Too much...

Rence snaps his eyes awake. Sleeping is bad, he knows that. He blinks, and the smudge in the near distance resolves itself into a rider. The snow is coming down too hard for him to make out any detail, and he still hopes that Jebediah Smith has returned to help him.

He cannot feel his left leg at all. If this situation suffers no change, he will die soon. He will fall asleep and the world will have seen the last of Rence Corness. He has to escape, get somewhere warmer, and that means – that means he has to do something desperate. Something that courses his veins with dread terror.

He grits his teeth and faces what he must do. He has to remove his leg so that the rest of him can be free. He tries to convince himself that since he can't feel the damn thing anyway, it will not hurt much. All he needs is his knife. His knife... oh God.

Oh well done, Lord, on this sweetest of ironies. The knife that he needs to remove his entrapping limb is thrust into his left boot, cosy alongside that limb itself. Underneath Red's immovable corpse, unreachable. Rence commences to laugh, a wheezing, hacking sound akin to a dying jackass. Although, he thinks, now that he has raised the Lord, he might just as well try prayer.

"Dear Lord," he stumbles, "I ain't used to talking to you. Hell, I ain't never talked to you, but I am now. I've been a thief and a bad egg in my time, but if you could see your way to uncrossing your legs and helping me out here, I'd be as thankful as a weasel in a hen house. Oh, it's me, by the way. Rence Corness."

Lord, give me strength here.

One more heave with his bent right leg then. He pours all his remaining strength into this push, muscles straining and veins standing out on his head. Not one damned inch does he move. God is a skunk, and no mistake.

Rence seriously considers shooting his leg off, but it would take who knew how many shots to cut through flesh and bone enough for him to leave the leg behind. Quite apart from which, although he has the Hawken near, he is not able to reach the cartridge pouch. He is going to have to think of another way out.

The indistinct rider continues a deliberate approach, slowly and steadily.

Rence was high above the world, head in the clouds. Red was moving slow, exhausted. It had been at least an hour since he'd shot the Injun, and he'd seen nothing behind whenever he'd checked. Once maybe he'd thought to spot her, and he'd loaded the Hawken, but it was only a rabbit scurrying away to God knew where. Maybe it was time for him to turn back. He was so bushed, mind, that a brief rest would more than help.

There was ice beneath the snow here. When he'd first heard the change in the sound of Red's hoofstrike he'd climbed down to investigate. Yup, ice, not rock.

Now what could lay ice on a slope, even such a shallow slant as this? An overflowed river? But there weren't no rivers up here were there, unless it was a baby one just starting out?

Ah hell, it didn't make no never mind anyways. The ice was strong and thick enough to support their weight, and that was all Rence cared about. They continued to move towards what he hoped was shelter.

A short way ahead of them a cliff-face rose sheer, taking the mountain to new heights. There was a jagged fissure in a fold of the hard rock wall. The space looked dark, deep; a cave mouth possibly. At the very least it would be enough to get him and Red out of the snow, which was still falling in great gobbets of frozen white.

His head nodded with weariness, and images of a hot saloon and the smell of sweat and cheap whisky drifted into his thoughts. He could almost hear the clank of the piano, the raucous laughter, the whore singing out of tune. He was already half asleep when the grizzly attacked.

It exploded at them out of the snowstorm like an avenging god, all dark fur and dark fury, enormous yellow teeth bared in an angry thunderous snarl. Before Red could react the bear sideswept his head with a massive paw, claws raking through the horse's face.

Red spun full about from the blow and fell heavily, dead before he hit the ground. Rence, still in the saddle and feet in the stirrups, yelled in agony as Red's full weight landed on his leg.

The grizz leapt onto Red's haunches, right behind Rence, and sank its teeth into horse-flesh. Rence felt the stinking breath of the bear warm his back as it feasted on Red's behind, jerking the body about as it tore at the haunch. In a matter of seconds the bear would move on to him.

Rence frantically tried to pull out the Hawken, whining in frustration as the barrel caught on the leather. He heaved on the stock and the gun came free.

He had but the one shot, his target was behind him, and he was lying on his left side. This would be a matter of sheer luck and guesswork. He held the rifle barrel under his right arm, aimed it at where he guessed the grizzly might be, tugged the trigger with his left thumb, and put his trust in fate.

The grizzly gasped and all movement stopped. Rence panted heavily, eyes panic-wide, listening for any sound of movement from behind him. There was only a soft hiss, as if a snow was being melted by something warm.

After a few minutes he began to calm down, and his breathing returned to normal. He was on his side, left leg trapped beneath his dead horse, facing back down the long way they'd come. This was rapidly turning into a day from hell.

The rider is the Crow woman. Of course it is. It has to be, naturally, on this day from hell. Her pony saunters up alongside Rence and she looks down at him, expressionless.

It is the woman he briefly saw naked the previous evening, her face like a burnt boot. Pine Leaf. She is wearing a decorated hide dress, leggings and moccasins. Her hair is tied in two braids, interwoven with crow feathers. The hair at the side of her head is matted with blood, and the front of her dress carries a bloody hole where Rence shot her.

She glances behind him.

"*Daxpitchée itbuuisée,*" she says.

"Yeah, I shot it," says Rence, feeling like he is hallucinating.

"You shot," Pine Leaf says, in English, indicating the hole in her dress.

"I did, and I'm sorry ma'am, I thought you were out to kill me dead. Now if you could just help me out of this pickle, you can have your pretty stick back and we can go our separate ways, no hard feelings, eh?"

"You shot. *Dúupe.* Try kill me dead."

"Heh, yeah, that I did. Which, by the way, you ain't. So how'd you manage that? What are you?" He hesitates to actually speak the word. "Immortal?"

"*Cheéta bia,*" she says, then at his frown "*loup-garou.*" She climbs down from her pony and kicks off her moccasins to stand barefoot in the snow. She reaches down for the hem of her dress and pulls it over her head, baring her breasts to the frozen air.

"Um, ma'am?" says Rence, beginning to suspect that the woman is soft in the head. "You sure you want to do that? Not that I ain't flattered and all, but it's mighty cold up here."

The woman thumbs down her leggings and steps out of them, standing unashamedly naked above him. Rence can't help but stare at the hair between her legs.

God damn.

"Ma'am?" Rence almost squeaks. What in tarnation is happening?

Pine Leaf squats beside him and dips her hand in the rivulet of blood by Rence's head. She puts her fingers to her mouth and licks the red from them, tongue slowly flicking her fingertips. She moves sideways to lean across him, full breasts hanging tantalisingly close to his face, then stands upright once more, now grasping the coup-stick that she has taken from his saddle bag. She kisses the eagle claw fixed to the end and moves the stick in circles above her head.

She shimmers, and her body wavers before Rence's eyes, almost as if it is melting. The proud breasts move in and up, and the hair between her legs spreads across the rest of her body. Her legs lengthen and bend unnaturally. She drops the coup stick and falls on all fours, arching her back as her face lengthens and her tail grows thick, furry and powerful.

Oh shit.

This is why she is formidable in battle. This is why she is such a good tracker. This is why Slitnose Jonah pissed his pants.

She prowls around the tableau of grizzly, horse and rider, growling low in her throat. Rence has heard of the Injuns singing death songs, and figures that he maybe might use this somehow to prolong his life by a few minutes. There is only one song he can bring to mind, and despite his terror he commences to sing it, haltingly, and with a sob in his voice. It is a song of a dying cowboy, of blood soaking into the hungry ground.

He is barely seven words in when the song is cut off by a terrible, heart-stopping scream that seems to last forever before it ends with a wet gurgle. Then the only sounds in the world are the soft fall of snow, the wet tearing of sharp teeth through flesh and bone, and a wolf's howl.

FERGUS

Fergus *was written as I sat on the lonely lookout point of Gamrie harbour in Scotland, gazing at a blood-red sun setting over the Moray Firth and watching small fishing boats, homeward bound, swing around the harbour wall by my feet.*

The light was fading rapidly now, sapphire to cobalt to indigo. The agreeable sunset apricot tint had faded from the clouds overhead and now they were simply battleship grey. The sea remained calm, but the surface began to chop as a cool breeze picked up, bringing the delicious scents of salt and seaweed to the shore. Gulls, waders and kittiwakes filled the dusk with their last raucous shrieks, whistles and mock laughter.

A maroon smudge smeared athwart the horizon was all that remained of the day's sun. In the near distance Saltire Craig, a small jut of rock no bigger than a trawler, rose black out of water the colour of molten lead. Pale grey smudges spattered its surface. They swirled and wheeled occasionally about the tattered *Bratach na h-Alba*, the Banner o' Scotland, that fluttered bravely atop its lonely pole, as it had since planted there by some hardy Scottish brave some time ago.

High on the lookout platform at the sea end of the harbour pier, Fergus eased his bony buttocks on the rusting bollard and stretched out his legs, feet poking out over the edge of the harbour wall. Inside his clumsy old boots he wiggled his toes, and imagined how good they'd feel with sea-water sluicing between them.

A loud splash echoed across the water, startling him. He peered into the murk, seeing nothing. The sound had originated from the other side of Saltire Craig, out of his sight. What could be large enough to make that noisy an impact with the water? Dolphins, perhaps? Or maybe old friends?

He gazed out at the ending day. Sunset always calmed his mind, soothed his soul, helped him to settle for the life he had now. On either side of the bay the headlands were already mussel-black. The vast dimming sky grew steadily darker.

Fifteen feet below his boots the waves lapped quietly at the weathered stone that protected the vessels safely tucked away behind it. More squealing gulls circled the end of the pier, curving pleasing arcs below his feet. Above his head a tiny red light winked on and began to flash.

A small white boat rounded Saltire Craig, its engine popping quietly as it crossed towards the harbour entrance. The boat was small, big enough only to carry two at most, yet now bearing but one passenger. Fergus could read the name painted on the prow – *"Maighdean-Chuain"*.

The single occupant raised a hand to Fergus as he passed and entered the placid waters beyond the sea wall. Fergus lifted his own arm in acknowledgement. It was good finally to feel included after all this time. His peculiar arrival in the village all those months ago had caused many to keep their distance at first, yet now even that extraordinary day was fading from memory. Village folk tended to live in the present rather than lingering on what was past. Folk here had finally started to show friendship to Fergus; yes, and acceptance. He scratched his grey beard and pulled the ear-flaps of his plaid charity-shop hat down over his ears. Getting chilly now.

He pushed to his feet, old muscles complaining. He wobbled a little in a gust of wind and steadied himself on the stanchion that held the harbour light aloft, before slowly descending the curved steps down from the lookout point.

He ambled along the dock to where the small boat had tied up, and peered down at it bobbing on the shadowy water.

There was enough light left to see that the man in the boat was gutting a freshly caught fish on an upturned blue crate. A sharp knife, expertly wielded, slit the belly open. Fingers were deftly inserted and slid smoothly inside to pull out the guts. These the fisherman flung into the water for the flocking, shrieking gulls to fight over. He glanced up at the dock.

"Fergus," the man nodded, laying his cleaned fish on a plastic bag beside him.

"Robbie Gamrie, is that you?" Fergus peered uncertainly down into the gloom.

"Aye, so," Robbie confirmed "Got mysel' a couple of late haddock."

Robbie lifted a second wriggling fish and whacked its head on the side of the boat before laying it on the blue crate and sliding in his knife.

"Well done, there," Fergus said. "What kept you out so late?"

"Forgetfulness. I was miles away, daydreaming like a bairn. I'd likely still be out there, but a noise brought me alert."

"The splash? Aye, I heard that. Big splash, it was. Did you see what made it?" Hope glimmered briefly in Fergus' breast.

"Nay, it was behind me, whatever it was."

"Hmm," said Fergus, slightly disappointed. "Too big for a bird, anyroad. Could it have been dolphins, think you?"

"Maybe. They... or silkies, eh?"

Fergus could hear Robbie's grin in the tone of his voice. Robbie didn't believe in silkies, despite the name of his boat. Not many did, nowadays.

"You'll have had your supper?" Robbie asked him.

"Ah, no. I'll have a rollie when I get in."

"Rollie be damned. You'll need warmth inside you if you've been perched up there for long. Here, catch."

A dark shape flew up from below to hover briefly before Fergus' eyes, shimmering a little in the harbour light. Fergus snatched out a hand to catch it before it fell back. The fish was cold and oily, the flesh yielding beneath his fingers as only fresh fish does.

"Got milk, Fergus? Butter and pepper? Get that inside your oven, then get it inside you. It'll do you a sight more good than cold bread."

"Thanks, laddie, I appreciate it." Fergus nodded farewell to Robbie and walked off the harbour, taking the shore path towards his tiny cottage, the haddock hanging limply from his fingers.

Fish for supper. He remembered a time long ago when supper had always been fresh fish. He did not eat it half as much these days, and the gift from Robbie was a pleasant surprise. Fergus was not inclined to take Robbie's advice on how best to prepare the haddock, however. He would not bake the fish in milk. Tonight he would eat the fish raw, just like the old days.

SALT

Salt *was knocked up in an idle hour after visiting the Hockney exhibition at Salts Mill, which was built by Titus Salt in the eighteen-fifties. This feels like the opening chapter of a longer story, and I may revisit it one day.*

Titus Salt alighted from his conveyance at Crow Nest Park and stretched out his long frame in relief. He breathed deeply of the fresh air, pleased to have left behind him the stench of the city for another day. George Weerth had the right of it when he had said *"If anyone wants to feel how a poor sinner is tormented in Purgatory, let him travel to Bradford."*

Salt's hound, a huge black beast the colour of his own hair, lolloped up to him and rested her big head against his leg in greeting. He ruffled the dog's ear, and gave her his newspaper to carry before striding towards the big front door of the mansion. He slowed down as he felt the cramp in his calves after a day on his feet.

"Come, Kanute!" he called to the dog, which happily trailed in his wake as he entered the large front door.

"Hello, the house!" he called, before remembering that his wife was away this day, taking their daughter Fanny to visit relatives in Harrogate. He laid down his hat and topcoat for the maid to find and clean later and ambled to his study.

He was delighted to find that the maid had already lit a fire in the grate. Kanute padded over to the rug on her great paws and sat before the warmth, dropping the soggy newspaper on the floor. A stuffed owl on the mantlepiece looked down on the dog disapprovingly.

The flames flickered merrily, their glow brightening the darkening room, their warm reflections dancing from the clutter of objects filling every corner. A telescope, a globe, inkwells on the desk, shelves groaning with books and geological samples, plants and stuffed birds – all the accoutrements that a successful gentleman might be expected to gather to him in Victoria's proud and prosperous realm.

Salt scratched Kanute's head, and the heavy tail thumped against the floor. He crossed to his desk and sat down. He opened a drawer and withdrew a rolled paper. He unrolled it across the desk, weighing it at either side with inkstand and blotter. He peered closely at the paper, lowering his head.

Hmmm. He twirled his greying beard between his fingers. Cheerful though the firelight was, the rich dark oak-paneled walls drank too much of the radiance before it reached him.

He returned to the fireplace and lighted a spill, carrying the flame back to the desk where he lit the Argand oil lamp. A soft yellow glow illumined the desk, driven by best colza oil. He sat down and looked again.

A section of the Aire Valley lay depicted before him. The area he had chosen for his new mill was fully three miles from Bradford's throttling stench. Surely people would work better in the clean air than in the centre of that stinking, breath-clogging hellhole.

He peered again at the map, trying to ascertain the exact boundary of the land that he had purchased. It was still too gloomy, and he sighed wearily.

"Though God Himself demand it, I cannot stand again," he thought.

He took up a heavy brass hand-bell and shook it vigorously, dispatching a loud summons through the house.

Shortly, the door opened and a maid entered. She was dressed in her working attire of dark ankle-length dress protected by a white pinafore. Her red hair was tied back, and her only adornment was a necklace from which depended a small silver skull. When he had first seen the necklace it had seemed to Salt a peculiar piece of jewellery for a young woman, but he was not one to hold harmless affectations against a person.

Kanute's tail thumped rhythmically against the rug as the maid entered. Kanute liked the maid. Indeed, Salt liked her too. She performed her duties well.

"You rang, sir?"

"Eileanora, yes," he replied, "Would you please light the candles? My legs seem to have decided to withdraw their labour."

"Yes, sir." Eileanora bobbed a quick curtsey and crossed to the fireplace, where she lit the several wicks of a candelabrum set on the mantlepiece in front of a mirror.

"Thank you," Salt said, "Perhaps you could also bring a pot of tea? And perhaps a dish of those delicious comfits from Harrogate?"

"Sir," she curtsied, and left the room. Salt turned his attention back to his plans. Perhaps if he could persuade Lady Rosse to sell him her land to the west, he might consider further building.

His train of thought was interrupted by Eileanora's knock at the door. For goodness sake, she had only just left.

"Yes?" he enquired, a little sharply.

The maid bobbed into the room once more.

"Begging your pardon, sir, but there are some gentlemen to see you."

"Who are they? Do they have cards?"

"No, sir. I did ask, but they wouldn't tell me who they were. Shall I fetch the groom, sir?"

Salt sighed deeply. He'd better go and see what they wanted. Perhaps they were workers looking for a job. He stood up with a groan.

"Very well, Eileanora, you can—"

The door behind the maid crashed open, sending her flying across the room. She sprawled across the floor by Kanute, who jumped up, barking loudly.

Three men burst into the study with a clattering of boots on the wooden floor. Kanute barked even more deafeningly.

"Shut that fucking dog up!" barked the ruffian at the front, brandishing a pair of pistols. The two with him each bore a knife and a club. Thieves! Desperate ones, too, if they had the nerve to break into a gentleman's house.

"There's no—" began Salt.

"Shut it!" ordered the one with the pistols. Salt took this as a sign that he was the leader of the trio. One of the others moved over towards Eileanora and pointed his knife at her.

"You shut that cur up now or I'll bash its brains in!" he snarled. The maid got to her feet, stroked Kanute, and spoke quietly to the dog. The barking ceased, though the dog sat alertly, watching carefully.

"There is very little money in the house," explained Salt.

"We don't want your money," spat the leader. He wore a brown jacket and trousers, neither of them displaying the threadbare appearance that one might expect of a ruffian thief. In fact, he did not have the appearance of a member of the working class at all.

"What do you want?" asked Salt.

"Well," said the man to the left, "*I* wouldn't mind availing myself of the maid service." He leered at the demure servant. She looked down at her feet, avoiding his gaze.

"Watch your manners," ordered the leader, and his henchman took a step back, chastened.

"Well now, Mr. Mayor," began the head ruffian, lowering his pistols, "You have been ruffling a few feathers lately. Very important feathers. For example, with all this claptrap that you've been trying to push through the council, trying to force a by-law to compel factory owners to use these expensive Smoke Burners."

"It would significantly improve the health of—"

"Bollocks it would," interrupted the intruder, "There's nowt wrong with a bit of smoke. Exercises the lungs, it does."

"I disagree," Salt argued. The leader of these men, at least, seemed quite articulate. Perhaps he would be open to reasoned argument.

"Might you be a medical man then, Mr. Salt?" enquired the intruder.

"I am not, as you must know. But I see all the cholera in the city. What causes that, pray, if not for filth, for grime, and a lack of clean air?"

"Lustful living," said the man, "Lustful urges and the drinking of cheap alcohol. That's my honest view, sir, but my honest view is not what matters. What matters is the view of my employers."

"I am no advocate of lustful living. I am no supporter of any sin, Mister..?"

"Chuff off. You don't need to know my name."

"Very well," Salt replied calmly, raising his hands to mollify the man. He'd been getting somewhere then, he was sure, but had put a foot wrong by asking the man's name. He should try to take this gently.

"I can see that you are a reasoning man," he began. "Come and look here, at these plans."

He beckoned the man over to his desk, where the Aire Valley map was spread out. The ruffian approached warily, though his pistols were held loosely at his sides now.

Salt indicated the area outlined in red ink.

"This is about three miles west of the city, along the Aire," he explained, "Mill workers here would have unsoiled air and clean living, and that, I maintain, can benefit not only the workers, but we owners, too. A happy worker is a good worker."

"According to my superior, who is paying me a great deal of money to visit you today, a happy worker is nothing of the sort. A happy worker is a worker who then imagines he has a *right* to that happiness. And once a worker has one right, he'll want others. Higher pay, more expensive housing, costly doctoring. Once the lower class gets a foothold, there'll be no stopping them."

The man's voice rose as he espoused thoughts obviously dearly held by himself as well as by his mysterious superior.

"I have evidence to the contrary," continued Salt, "From my own woollen mills. I have fitted the Rodda Smoke Burners. I therefore have a healthier workforce. They are sick less often, for a start."

"And it cost you a packet, didn't it? These burners are expensive things. You might be able to afford such doings, but others cannot. You just desire to drive others out of business so that you can obtain their mills for yourself and grow your empire. I know greed, and I see right through your fancy words, Mr. Salt!"

"But I...." Salt paused, unsure of how to proceed in the face of this man's rising anger, then continued, trying to keep his voice calm.

"Look, what would you say if I told you that I will soon build a new mill in this place." He swept his hand across the map, "Out in the countryside, where I can properly test my hypothesis. Perhaps even houses, with running water on tap from the river? What would you say then?"

"I'd say that you've signed your own death certificate, Mr. Mayor."

The man's lip curled, and he pushed Salt back down into the desk chair. He raised a pistol and pressed the barrel against Salt's forehead. Salt stared up wide-eyed at the anger in the man's twisted face and prepared to meet his God.

A narrow beam of pale blue light shone out of the man's left eye, and the eyeball melted. The beginning of a scream was cut off as the light swept through the face, slicing away the top of the man's head.

As the body of his assailant fell away and the pistols clattered to the floor, the figure of Eileanora was revealed to Salt. She stood erect, a determined look on her face. Her right arm was outstretched, and in her hand was a bizarre device from which emerged the thin beam of blue light.

Her left hand gripped the throat of one of the henchmen, and as Salt gazed on aghast, a simple twist of her wrist dispatched him from this life. His corpse fell to the floor. Kanute yipped approvingly.

The thin blue light swept inexorably across the room and sliced into the third man's chest. He too fell lifeless, tumbling like one of Fanny's rag dolls.

Eileanora touched her skull necklace with her left forefinger and spoke.

"Hey, it's Tabby. I'm done here. Extraction, please."

She *shimmered*, then simply disappeared, her maid's uniform falling still warm to the floor as it was left behind.

VALENTINE

Valentine *is a love story. No, really, it is.*
Trust me, I'm a wombat. I wrote it for Lisa
Shambrook's "Love Bites" flash fiction challenge,
but here I have loosened it a little from the tight
corset of its word-count constraints so that it is a
much smoother read.

Such a perfect blue, those eyes. Gareth gazed into them, certain that she was the one. The corners of her faultless mouth dimpled. He stroked her waist, and squeezed her fingers with his other hand as they swayed to the seductive rhythm of *'Moonlight Serenade'*. As the music ended, he brushed her ear with his lips.

"Will you be my Valentine?" he whispered.

"If you'll be mine," she smiled, those amazing eyes twinkling.

"Come up to my room?"

She bit her lip, and glanced nervously at the other dancers, as if they might have heard. She nodded.

"But come to mine. I shall be able to relax more. And *only* for a quiet drink."

She gave a stern look. He had better not frighten her with over-enthusiasm.

"I cannot promise not to kiss you, you have beguiled me so. We can stay here, if you feel safer."

Marian dimpled one side of her tempting mouth in a wry grin and raised a mischievous eyebrow.

"Perhaps just *one* kiss."

Bingo. He had been right to target this shy little wallflower rather than one of the more confident women here. An innocent conquest was far more exciting.

Marian took his hand and gazed up at him. He led her between the gyrating couples and out to the wide staircase. Her ball gown rustled tantalisingly. He pictured what her legs might look like above those delicate ankles, and thoughts of what lay higher set his pulse racing. He would love to be the first explorer of those hidden hills and valleys.

She paused at her door.

"I'm not one of those easy girls, you know," she said, quietly.

"That's why I fell for you, darling. Your purity of spirit." *Blah blah blah.*

Her room was luxurious; radiogram, sofa, even a bar. Bedroom to the right, he noted.

"Can you find some decent music?" she asked, trembling. "I can't work the radio at all."

The machine hummed softly as it warmed up. He found a station playing swing music, all the while gazing at her slight figure, hands clasped in front of her like a shield. Time to clinch the deal.

"Marian," he said. She lifted her eyes like a timid doe. "I don't want you to feel compelled to do anything that you don't want." *Oh yeah, lay it on, boy.* "But I have fallen deeply for you. Fate arranged our meeting on this special night. The night of true love, of Saint Valentine."

She gave a little smile, and relaxed her bare shoulders.

"Turn the music up, please?" she asked, "It relaxes me."

Excellent. He would have her this night, whether she wanted it or not, and would prefer if no-one heard her screams. He twisted the dial and Benny Goodman filled the room.

"Would you...?" she faltered.

"Anything, my Valentine."

"Would you make us a drink? While I..." she gestured behind her, to the bedroom. He nodded, and began to mix drinks at the bar. Behind him Marian stepped into the bedroom, babbling nervously.

"Do you know much about Saint Valentine?" she asked.

"No, I'm afraid not. Do you?"

"Some," she said, lifting the baseball bat from the bed.

"Tell me."

She eased off her shoes and stepped back through the door.

"Saint Valentine was actually two men, who have over time become joined into one legend."

"Really? How fascinating." Jesus, he couldn't wait to shut up her babble.

She crossed the room, the deep carpet tickling her toes. "Different men, but they both met the same end. And now, my love, you are *my* Valentine."

She swung the bat violently into his right leg, shattering the bones of his knee. He crumpled with a scream, writhing on the floor. Benny Goodman picked up the tempo.

"They were beaten with clubs," she explained, arcing the bat to shatter his other knee. She thrust the end of the bat hard into his genitals.

"Of course, that's not what killed them," she continued calmly, swinging the bat above her head and down hard across his stomach. He vomited, and sobbed.

"The clubs merely immobilised them, like this," she explained, and with a cheerful smile splintered bones in both his arms.

"No," she said, taking a knife from the bar. "What killed them was being beheaded alive."

THE LUCK OF EDEN HALL

This is my rather poor attempt at writing in the style of old English balladeers. The story is based on a fairy legend of Cumberland; in particular on a ballad of the same name written in 1826 by a man by the splendid name of Jeremiah Holmes Wiffen.

On Eden's wild romantic bowers the summer moonbeams sweetly fell, and tinted with yellow light the stately towers of Eden Hall. There, lonely in the deepening night, a lady at her lattice sat and trimmed her taper's wavering light. She tuned her idle lute by fits, but little could it beguile the weary moments now. Neither lay, nor song, nor verse seemed to suit her wistful eye and anxious brow, for as her finger swept the chord, oft-times she checked her simple song to chide the forward chance that kept Lord Musgrave from her arms. Lady Edith listened, as the wind swept the ancient stones, eager to hear his steed's familiar step.

"Wait! What sound is that? Peace, beating heart, twas but the cry and footfall of a distant deer." Lady Edith fancied then that she heard an echoed whisper on the perfumed breeze, a verse borne by the wind for her ears alone:

In, lady, to thy bower; fast weep
The chill dews on thy cheek so pale;
Thy cherished hero lies asleep-
Asleep in distant Rossendale!

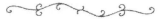

The afternoon had been sultry, and the chase long. The wild stag eyed Lord Musgrave and his dog, Ben, from across a leafy glade, its face reflecting the purple light of the dying day.

"My Lord?" questioned the boy from astride his shaggy little pony.

"It's mocking us, Gladstone, do you see?" The stag slowly faded into the twilight.

"My Lord, we have strayed far from home," young Gladstone gave in worried tone, "Through many a dale must we hie; up many a hill must our mounts strain e'er we behold with gladsome eye your verdant bowers again."

"You have the right of it, lad. The twilight deepens. Oe'r the wolds the yellow moonbeam rising plays with shadow, and now the haunted forest holds the wanderers in its bosky maze."

"You mean we're lost in the forest after dark? I fear you are right, my Lord, and we must forego the home-felt comforts of Musgrave Towers this night for the grassy ground of Rossendale."

"It becomes too dark to move through wood. Let us sleep here, on this green bank; the night will be warm." They tied their steeds to a nearby alder, and Lord Musgrave flung himself down on the greensward. A prayer and a sigh in murmurs faint he whispered to the passing air. The prayer was an *Ave* to his patron saint. The sigh was to his lady fair.

It was well that in that elfin wood he breathed the supplicating charm which binds the guardians of good to shield those who pray from unearthly harm. Scarce had the night's pale Lady Moon stayed her chariot oe'r the leafy oak than he was nudged awake by his boy.

"Wake, Lord!" Gladstone hissed, "Listen!"

Low murmurs echoed in the mystic shade beyond their grassy bank. The manes of both horse and pony stiffened with dread. Ben, crouching low, whined and quaked the wild fern around him as though some passing ghost were near.

The moon calmly cast her pale light on glade and hillock, flower and tree, and sweet the nightingale poured forth her music, wild and free. All seemed normal, save for that unearthly murmur.

Then the nightingale's notes fell hushed, and close nearby flutes began to breathe. Horns warbled, and the Lord and his boy, in shadow hid, heard the ringing of bridles and pounding of hooves. They crept forward and peered around the old oak. The sight they beheld drew their breath away.

In gay cavalcade from out the wood appeared the fairies round their fairy king. A hundred elfin knights and more were there in silk and steel arrayed. Each wore a ruby helmet, and each bore a diamond lance. Pursuivants with wands of gold there were, too, and minstrels scarfed and laurelled fair. They saw heralds with blazoned flags unrolled and trumpet-tuning dwarves. Behind these, scores of ladies coy on milk-white steeds brought up their queen; their kerchiefs were of crimson, their kirtles of an argent sheen. Some wore, in fanciful costume, a sapphire or a topaz crown, some a hern's or peacock's plume which their own tercel falcons had struck down. Masked, some were, and others hooded or turbaned. They had bound their undulating hair with sweet-smelling woodbine from the forest.

The company's bright tints caused the darksome shade of the forest to grow florid as they passed; all sounds of bird and creature from amongst the trees tuned themselves to the elfin song. They slowed their march nearby, and quit their steeds. The knights advanced and in quaint order, one by one, each led a lady forth to dance. The timbrels sounded and the fairy magic began.

Where'er they tripped, where'er they trod, a daisy or a bluebell sprang. Cowslips, poppy and campion blue were there also. Leaves on trees above the dancers glowed with a verdant light, illuminating the festival below. As Lord Musgrave and Gladstone watched entranced, the fairy dancers commenced a rousing song.

Lord Musgrave, head a-tilt, smiled broadly at the joysome music despite the fears that rose in his chest. Gladstone crept forward to get a better view, as the minstrelsy declined. The dancers stilled, and shawms resounded a clarion throughout the wood. Beneath the shining leaves ranks of heralds formed, and between them walked a lady of utmost beauty, the crown atop her tumbling tresses almost piercing the illumined leaves.

"Titania!" whispered Gladstone.

"I beg your pardon?"

"Titania - the Fairy Queen! The king there, that's Oberon." Gladstone's eyes sparkled with excitement.

Titania waved her crystal wand as she moved, and where she went beneath the greenwood bower tables, urns and goblets appeared. So too metheglin, nectar, fruits and flowers appeared upon the groaning tables.

"To banquet!" called Oberon.

"To banquet!" echoed his smiling queen.

"To banquet, ho!" the seneschals bid the brisk tribes of fairy that, as thick as bees, at the sound of cymbals gathered to the tables beneath the leafy trees. Titania stood by her king, each knight beside his lady love, each page behind his escutcheoned lord. It was a sight of such extravagant colour that it mesmerised the secret watchers. The monarch

Oberon sat, and all helms were doffed; plumes, scarves and mantles were cast aside to the verdant ground. To the sound of music soft the fairies plied their cups with much delight. Of sparkling mead they drank; of spangling dew, or livelier hypocras they sipped. Strawberries red and mulberries blue refreshed each elf's luxurious lip. Mirthful airs crowned the festive gathering as the revellers heaped their jewelled patines high.

A minstrel dwarf, in silk arrayed, meandered o'er to lie on a mossy bank near where the unseen watchers lay. Wild thyme wove its fragrant braid beneath him, whilst violet spread its rich perfume. As a page at Oberon's knee presented high a wassail cup of enamelled glass, the little bard raised up his harp of ivory and sang a lay concerning the goblet thus presented. The dwarf sang merrily to the health of his sovereign; the song also told that the goblet would ensure health and good fortune. Joy also would it bring the bearer from its charmed rim. He sang that the goblet had been wrought within a wizard's mould, and held within it charms and spells to ensure good luck and happiness to whomsoever owned it. The fairy band rose to their feet, and the wild wood echoed to their myriad toast: "Health to our king by wold and rill! Health to our queen in bower and hall!"

Lord Musgrave's eyes narrowed, and an errant thought fired his mind.

"Hold Ben here, Gladstone," he told the young lad by his side.

"Wait, no—" Gladstone began, and rose to prevent his Lord's rash intent. Too late was he, and he stood helpless as

Lord Musgrave dashed across the lush green bank and hurdled the dwarven harper.

"So help me all the powers of light!" cried the noble Lord as he rushed into the festal train and snatched up the goblet bright directly from the king's hand, along with a silver spoon from the table.

"Loose the steeds!" Lord Musgrave yelled, and to frantic barking from Ben, Gladstone untied horse and pony from the alder tree and clambered onto his pony's back, turning to see what unfolded. There was uproar all around and behind Lord Musgrave; screaming Fays leapt to their saddles, or loosed shafts of death from their bows.

"The charmed cup is lost!" bellowed Oberon, "Stretch to the strife, fay warriors! Away, away!" With five brave bounds Lord Musgrave crossed the ground. The sixth took him by the minstrel dwarf, whom he knocked to the ground with a mighty blow. The seventh sat him upon his steed. Arrows whipped by them, cleaving the once joyful air.

"Now, Ace!" cried Musgrave to his steed, "Faster fly than the wind, or thy master is lost!" Ace sprang forward immediately, taking the breath from Lord Musgrave, while behind him Queen Titania cried "Do not let them reach the stream! If they cross it the cup is lost!"

"Keep up, young Gladstone!" cried the exhilarated lord.

"Yes, my L—AAAAH!" came from behind him. From the corner of his eye he could see that Gladstone's pony, a brave and stalwart beast, yet kept pace with Ace's strides, and so he concentrated on avoiding the close-packed trees. As in a whirlwind the fairy hordes careered after them, the turf trembling as they passed. Forward still thrust Lord Musgrave and Gladstone. An elven arrow bounced off the cup in Lord Musgrave's left hand, but he managed to retain his grip. The spoon he gripped tight between his teeth.

"Here's the stream ahead, my brave page," he encouraged young Gladstone, "Once on t'other side we're safe!" Scores of archers rained their shafts about them as they splashed through the shallow water, but as they reached the further bank the arrows ceased to buzz around their ears. Ace panted heavily. A fairy arrow protruded from his haunch, but the brave horse stood firm and true. Gladstone, however, was not so stalwart, and slid from his gasping pony's back in a faint, his face coated with gore. Lord Musgrave leapt from his horse and filled the fairy goblet from the stream. He knelt by Gladstone's side and laid the lad's head on a mossy tussock. The crystal water from the fairy cup washed away most of the blood to reveal the horror that had been done to Gladstone's face by a fairy arrow.

"You've lost your nose, my brave boy, but you will heal. And I shall fashion for you a new nose from the fairy spoon." Gladstone heard little of this, residing as he did in a dreamless sleep.

"Joy to thy banner, bold Sir Knight!" came a bellow from the opposite bank. Oberon sat astride a jet-black charger, his beard bristling. He raised a hand in salute. "Heed my warning, however. If yon goblet break or crack, farewell to your vantage in fight and in life. Farewell to your fortune and riches. Your house will fall into utter ruin."

The forest cleared. Lord Musgrave looked down on Gladstone's ruined face. The water from the chalice had stemmed the bleeding, and seemed to have numbed pain, for the boy slept soundly. Ben licked at his cheek in concern.

"Come, Ben," said Lord Musgrave. "Let's go home."

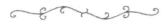

Twas dusk of the following day; in Musgrave Towers Lady Edith bent o'er her infants and listened to the faint tinkling that ascended from the gift that Lord Musgrave had brought her; a cup of richly enamelled glass.

"List, Eleanor," she whispered, "List, Catherine! Hear your father's wondrous gift to you and your children."

"Sleep sweetly, babes," the goblet sang, but softly, "All good things be thine this day. Yet if this goblet break or crack, farewell thy vantage in the fray. Farewell the Luck of the Musgraves." The young sisters slept on.

Though year upon year has taken flight since that day, good fortune is still the Musgrave's thrall. Raise now your glasses, and drink a toast to the vantage of the Musgraves, the fortune of the Musgraves, and most of all, the Luck of Eden Hall.

DANCING AT WHITSUN

A favourite song of mine is Austin John Marshall's 'Dancing at Whitsun'. I first heard the song performed by Maddy Prior and Tim Hart in those far off days before even Steeleye Span existed. This short story of a Whitsuntide dance was inspired by that song.

A thrill shivered through Jeannie as she felt the touch of Gordon's hand on hers. He lightly stroked the back of her fingers, causing the fine hair on her forearms to stand on end.

The fiddlers outside the pub struck up *"The Nutting Girl"*. Gordon bowed, and drew her into a lively stepping dance. Her new white linen dress flowed about her nimble ankles, the green ribbons in her dark hair dancing a lively jig of their own as the couple whirled in happy enjoyment across the village green. As the tune ended, the other couples clapped and laughed, but Gordon took her hands in his and bent to kiss her gently.

"Marry me?" he whispered.

"Yes, oh yes," said Jeannie eyes moistening. "I'll always be yours. You have my heart forever, you know that."

"I know..." he said, hesitantly, "I know too that my unit leaves tomorrow. I have to go. But I will return." He squeezed her hands, his grey eyes full of promise. "Nothing can stop me being with you. I will return, and we will be married next Whitsun, if you think it not too long a wait?"

"We first met last Whitsuntide," she smiled "Our special time. Oh, that will be perfect!" She flung her arms around his neck and kissed him full on the lips. The crowd of villagers around them burst into spontaneous applause.

Twenty yards away Mrs. Bickerdike and Mrs. Lowry leaned on the latter's garden fence, looking out onto the village green, which held a lone figure. They watched Jeannie as she clasped her hands together in delight and nodded joyfully, gazing up at nothing with a huge smile on her wrinkled face. Then, slowly, though there was no music, the old woman moved her feet, treading as gentle a measure as age would allow across the lush grass. Her bare feet were stained as green as the tattered ribbons threaded in her sparse white hair. Her gaunt arms encircled the thin air.

"What's that old bint faffing about at?" asked Mrs. Lowry. "Is she a bit doolally?"

"Oh aye, you won't know. This is your first Whitsun here, isn't it?"

"It is. We flitted in '90, and we were away in Filey the last couple of years. Why, what's to do?"

"That there's Nutting Jeannie," Mrs. Bickerdike told her, adjusting her pinny across her ample bosom.

"She is nuts then?"

"Nay. Well, aye, happen, but that's not where she gets that name. If you listen close when she dances you can hear her humming a tune – 'The Nutting Girl' it's called. That's why folk call her Nutting Jeannie."

"Never heard of it."

"Aye, well, it's an old tune. Sithee, fifty year back there were allus a Whitsun dance on the green. Girls'd get dressed pretty, be-ribbon their hair, and dance with their beaux. Came the war, and all the young men went off to be wasted in battle – husbands and brothers and fathers and sons. And fiancés."

"Her fiancé?"

"Aye, Jeannie's young man. Their last day together was the Whitsun Dance in 1942, just afore the last few village men went off to do their duty. Her young man – Gideon, I think – announced their engagement in The Royal Oak that evening. Next day he went off and were blown to smithereens in France."

"Chuffing hell, the poor bugger."

"Aye. It devastated Jeannie, of course. And you know, she never looked at another man. Oh, her parents tried to get her interested from time to time, but she'd have none of it. She'd given her heart to Gideon, and no bugger else was worthy of it."

"Poor cow," decided Mrs. Lowry.

"Aye. Anyroad, every Whitsun since that she's put that ragged white dress on and danced on the green. Rain or shine, she'll be there, dancing with her invisible lover. Still doing it now, see? Still waiting for her man to come home again."

"Definitely doolally, then. Lost her marbles."

"Mebbe so, but don't you think it's dead romantic? Staying faithful to her one true love for half a century?"

"No, I bloody don't." Mrs. Lowry sniffed. "God knows how she's managed all that time without a man to warm her nethers."

"Aye, well, not everybody's sex-mad like—oh my God!"

Jeannie had crumpled to the warm ground, and now lay awkwardly. A soft breeze tugged at the ragged hem of her dress, and one scrawny arm moved falteringly in the air.

Mrs. Bickerdike and Mrs. Lowry ran across to her and knelt at her side.

"Jeannie, love, are you alright?"

The old woman looked up at Mrs. Bickerdike, a worried expression on her face.

"Where's Gordon?" she creaked, her voice like sandpaper on skin.

"I don't know a Gordon, love."

"He'll come," Jeannie sighed, barely audible now. "He promised. He'll..."

The wrinkled old lips emitted a gasp, and a horrible rattle. A light left her rheumy eyes, and they stared blankly up at the scudding clouds.

Mrs. Bickerdike gently lowered Jeannie's eyelids so that the dead eyes were covered.

"She's gone," she said, sadly.

Jeannie ignored her. She did not care. She and Gordon were strolling hand-in-hand in Spring sunshine through groves of white blossom, by fields of young corn, to the forest of oak trees at the end of the lane.

FLIGHT

A tale based on real characters and actual events from the early days of flying before the First World War, when Filey in East Yorkshire was home to a flying club that operated from the beach near Primrose Valley. I have fiddled with the order of events slightly for dramatic purposes.

.

The wind whipped Hubert Oxley's hair about his ears. He whooped with exhilaration. He had to be travelling at almost fifty miles per hour. Dare he push further? Boldly, he twisted the throttle and nudged the sixty horsepower Renault engine to give him just a little more speed. Three hundred feet below his Mercury III the people of the small town of Filey, mostly summer tourists making the most of the early evening sun, gazed up at him open-mouthed. He slowed and circled the lofty spire of the Wesleyan Chapel. As he pulled out of the turn he cheerfully waved at a young lad gawping up at him from the street below.

His wheels barely clearing the hot slate roofs of the houses he headed toward the cliffs. So ecstatic was he to be skimming the wind that he determined once more to enjoy the thrill of his favourite manoeuvre. The sea ahead twinkled cheerful encouragement. As he reached the cliff top, he pushed the nose of the aircraft steeply down into a dive over the edge. His stomach flip-flopped. He knew that he had but three hundred feet of cliff to play with, and that was not much. He also knew, however, the capabilities of Mr. Blackburn's new monoplane. With exquisite timing he heaved on the column, canvas flapped loudly, cottonwood wing-ribs twisted, and the aircraft flattened out, its tyres skimming the beach. He allowed the Mercury to drift gently onto the firm sand and trundle to a halt. He turned off the engine, clambered over the empty passenger seat, and jumped down, sighing happily.

Two figures jogged towards him across the sweltering beach. Effie, her long white dress swinging, her dark hair bouncing, reached him several yards ahead of the puffing Weiss.

"Married three days and you try to kill yourself!" she shrieked, swatting at him with a huge, feathery hat. Hubert laughed, which merely brought him another ineffectual blow as Effie gave vent to her obvious anger. Other emotions crossed that beautiful face too, he realised. Concern. Concern in the way her mouth curved, and yes, love in her hazel eyes.

"And where's your helmet?" she continued, "If you hit a gull you could be blinded or something!"

"The birds know to get out of my way, and it's far too hot for wrapping one's head in leather."

"I had thought," she continued, "that on our honeymoon at least, you might give up on these silly jaunts; these juvenile frolics on what is no more than a large boys' toy, a new-fangled fashionable bagatelle."

Bob Weiss finally arrived, breathing hard. As he reached them he caught Effie's sharp tone and swiftly turned on his heel towards the tail of the aircraft, rolling his eyes and smiling at Hubert's discomfort.

"You might think flying new-fangled," tried Hubert, "and yes, the breakthrough of *powered* flight was not seven years ago when Orville Wright took his Flyer up for twelve seconds on a different beach, but the first ever *manned* flight was over fifty years back, and in Yorkshire, too. It is not a passing fad, darling; flight is here to stay."

"Rubbish. It's not natural. Who but a madman would want to go aloft in one of those draughty contraptions?"

"Anyone who craves excitement! You would find it a breathtaking experience, my sweet, I'll warrant."

"Balderdash, Hubert."

"My dear, you criticise that of which you have no experience."

"Oh, no, I'm not falling for that one. Not a chance."

"Bob!" Hubert called Weiss over. "Tell Effie that she has to fly with me. She has to feel the wind lift her and raise her above the birds, or she will never understand the bliss of flight."

"True it is, Mrs. Oxley," Weiss told her, his speech still heavily accented despite six years in England. "Flying is... is pure joy. I do advise you to give it a go. It is a remarkable experience. Also, if you do not, you will never win this argument with your stubborn husband."

Hubert bowed in concession of this description. He took his wife's hand and said "Come with me, Effie. Let me show you what it's really like!"

"Stubborn, indeed. Oh... very well," she agreed. It was undeniable that any future argument that she might attempt against Hubert's strange desire to get off the ground would founder on her lack of personal experience. She was reluctant to admit that there was also a small part of her that was attracted by the idea, of engaging in an activity that few of her gender would even contemplate, even if their men folk saw fit allow it. "When shall we go?"

"Why not now?"

"But it is not long until sunset. And the tide?"

"Not to worry, the tide will give us an hour yet. Fires, Bob?"

Weiss nodded, and moved to lift the tail of the Mercury. Hubert helped him turn the aircraft so that it pointed along the beach, while Effie watched anxiously, chewing on a finger. What had she agreed to? Look at the thing – it was no more than a few sticks and sheets of cloth screwed and glued around an engine. She could not imagine how something heavier than the air could possibly rise above it. When she had asked Hubert, he had blathered on about wing-shapes and air-flow, but had spoken so rapidly in his enthusiasm that she had not been able to follow. She was suddenly very nervous.

Yet she could not back out of her agreement now without appearing a timid, demure female, and she hated that image of her sex. No; she would have to endure this one flight now that she had agreed. At least it would give weight to her future insistences that her husband give up flying.

She allowed Hubert and Weiss to assist her into the cramped passenger seat, which took some time due to her light summer attire and the need for modesty. She handed Weiss her hat, to look after until her return, together with an admonition not to act the silly fool by wearing it.

Hubert jumped into the pilot's seat behind her. The engine puttered into life, startling a nearby flock of seagulls into flight, squealing their annoyance. The sky was beginning to darken as the sun dipped below the cliffs that loomed on their left. To the right, leisurely advancing waves sussurated in the near distance. Ahead of them, across the bay, the dark bulk of Filey Brigg flung itself out into the sea.

With a start Effie realised that they were moving, slowly at first, but swiftly picking up speed. The aircraft's progress along the beach was surprisingly smooth. She would have thought that rocks, or even undulations in the sand, might make the going a little bumpy, but... oh!

No wonder the ride was smooth. They were already airborne. The cliffs fell away on the left and revealed a deep, glorious sunset across the distant fields. Effie suddenly realised that she had been holding her breath and released it with a loud gasp. She gripped the hand-rail before her and turned her attention ahead, peering through the blur of the propeller. There rose the bulk of the Brigg, but amazingly they were already higher than that. The old town passed beneath them, and she marvelled at the tiny figures on the Coble Landing, the gulls passing beneath her feet, and the wind buffeting her cheeks.

This was a sublime sensation. The insubstantial air carried the flimsy craft as surely as a mother's arms, and... oh, the view ahead! The coast stretched into the far distance, curving in and out of bays like the scalloped collar of her dress, lined by the pale stitch of breaking waves. Effie was captivated. No wonder Hubert had insisted on returning to this unnatural element, this incredible sensation time and time again. She felt like a Goddess.

As the blue above darkened, she determined that she herself would from henceforth also be a regular denizen of the air. Perhaps Hubert might even teach her how to control this miracle of engineering.

A cluster of pale lights ahead marked their arrival at a town. On the headland above it the silhouette of a castle stood against the indigo sky. Scarborough. So far, in so little time? It was scarcely believable.

Hubert took them around a gentle turn above the boat-bobbing harbour and they headed back down the coast, occasional lights from cottages and crofts now beginning to spatter the dark land. Across the sea a pale half moon glowed, and Effie felt that this must be what heaven was like. The enjoyment burst out of her loudly in a rendition of the popular song of the day;

Come Josephine in my flying machine
Going up she goes, up she goes.

Above the growl of the engine she could hear Hubert's laughter from behind. The scoundrel, he had known that she would love this. Why had he not made her come up with him before? He was in for a severe nagging when they landed. A short strip of yellow appeared ahead which puzzled her for a moment, until she realised the scale of what she was seeing.

Bonfires! Weiss had lit a line of fires to guide them home and to illuminate their landing ground. Amber light flooded a wide strip of sand from the cliffs to the approaching tide. Hubert, however, first turned inland and circled the chapel tower, before again approaching the beach, this time from the dark land.

The very moment that the fires on the beach appeared above the cliff edge, the aeroplane plunged into a steep dive, and to Effie the world began to move in slow motion. She remembered his thrilling landing earlier, flying vertically down the cliff-face before levelling out and gently settling onto the sand. Her stomach tightened with excitement. The lip of the cliff, a dark scar against ochre-lit sands, passed their wheels as they sped downward. The wind tore at her hair. They must be travelling at over a hundred miles per hour by now. She began a scream of joyful excitement just as the right wing tear away from the fuselage. Fabric covering the flimsy airframe beside her shredded and ripped away, flying into the night like ribbons in a gale. The wing-strut to her left cracked apart and flew backwards. Her face now a grimace of horror she watched as the propeller hit the sand, churning into it briefly before the aircraft toppled and she was flung into the air, flying this time without the aid of machine. The universe was a whirling vortex of fires, yellow light, running figures and crashing waves. Then the universe was black.

"The airframe could not accept such stress, *verstehen?*" Weiss told her, "It tore apart. I think that you must have been descending at a hundred and fifty miles per hour when into the ground you hit."

Effie said nothing, but stared at the white-clad pierrots prancing on the hot sand, and at the summer crowds enjoying their holiday entertainment not fifty yards from where her husband had died just a week before. She ran her finger along the wickerwork of the bath chair in which she sat, enjoying the tactile sensation. The weave reminded her of the ripples on sand after the sea had retreated from it.

"Would you like an ice?" Weiss asked her. She was unmoving, silent. "Ah, so," he continued, leaning back into his deckchair again. "You will speak when you are ready and good, so said Dr. Beckett."

A sea breeze lifted Effie's chestnut hair. It caressed her cheeks, and she felt almost as though she rise from the dull earth and join the gulls overhead. The pierrots sang *'Come Josephine in my Flying Machine'*.

"I shall have to take you back to the sanatorium now," said Weiss, "Mr. Blackburn has today a party from Leeds that have booked a pleasure flight, and now that we are a pilot short—"

"Mr. Weiss?" Effie gave voice for the first time in seven days, "Will you teach me how to fly?"

TOOTH AND CLAW

Written for Anthology Clubs forthcoming 'Dragonthology' collection, this tale was at various times called both 'Flossaraptor' and 'Molar Expedition', both of which you will understand after the first page. Thank goodness I eventually saw the light and avoided such agonising puns.

"Open a little wider, please," Jena said. Her patient complied willingly, allowing her to reach the rearmost molar. She tapped the enamel with the sickle probe, then tilted the mirror slightly the better to see behind the tooth. It was fine, although fully as much in need of a clean as the others. She counted the lower teeth out clearly as she checked them, so that her assistant Susi could make proper notes.

"Ten, nine, eight, seven, six, five missing, four-three-two-one," she enumerated the right lower jaw. She moved on to the left side, beginning with the front teeth. "One-two-three, four slight occlusion, five, six, seven, eight missing, nine, ten," she reported.

"OK, I've got all that," called Susi.

"Then by the Ancestors help me to get out of here. It stinks to high heaven."

She handed out the probe and mirror first, which Susi leaned against the wall of the cavern before stretching out a hand. Jena took it, grateful for the support as she swung her lags over the double-row of huge teeth. As her feet gratefully settled on solid ground, there was a guttural rumble from above and the immense creature behind her let out a gust of breath that stank of ordure, decay and rot. Jena and Susi tensed for a moment, but thankfully there was no heat in that fetid wind.

"Well?" an acid voice resonated from above their heads. The Dark Queen tilted her head to peer down at them from a massive, multi-faceted eye. She adjusted her mighty wings with a rustle like a shower of acorns on a windy day. In the dim light of the cavern her bark-like, brown-green skin looked almost black. The wings that were attached to her forelimbs were fringed with dark green needles that she could use to inflict deep cuts on those who displeased her. She was covered with imbricate woody scales that overlapped each other like those of a fish, and were spirally arranged about her body. As the Dark Queen heaved her bulk around, the individual scales rippled and rasped against each other.

"Did you not hear your queen, hominid?" demanded the dragon. Susi nudged Jena urgently.

"Yes," Jena said, hastily. "My apologies, Queen Daf'q. I was merely catching my breath. There's a slight malocclusion - erm, your bite does not quite meet correctly - on the left in the back row, but you don't need to worry about it unless it worsens. All in all, there's nothing amiss with your teeth that a good clean won't fix. Your majesty might consider getting a hygienist in there to give everything a good clean."

"Your hygienist, it will do it now," ordered the Dark Queen.

"Majesty, Susi here is no hygenist. She is my assistant, here to take notes and to help me safely in and out of your impressive mouth. Neither she nor I have the skill to undertake a proper cleaning task. You may... you may remember eating my usual hygienist at our last appointment?"

"Ah yes," the dragon nodded. "It was crunchy, with a tang of peppermint. Very well. You will do it yourself."

"I do not have the necessary equipment with me. I—"

"Do not test my patience, hominid!" bellowed the magnificent dragon, bathing them once again in the rich odour of rotting meat. "You will bring your equipment on the morrow, and you will clean my teeth."

"Yes, majesty," Jena agreed quickly. Susi hid as best she could behind Jena.

"Now you may leave me. Return to the wall, where a Bryo awaits to take you to your village. Warn it that you will return on the morrow."

"Yes, majesty." Jena waited for a moment, but the dragon queen already seemed have forgotten them, resting her massive head on her mighty-clawed feet before closing her eyes. Jena and Susi tiptoed out of the vast cavern into watery sunlight.

They stood on a high ledge overlooking a flat plain. The rock face from which they had emerged stretched to left, right, and above as far as they could see. Scores of openings, of various sizes, spattered the cliff face, though none were as large as the one that they had just left. Dragons of various sizes left or entered these apertures, cleaving the air above their heads. Dark green Pteros and yellow Bryo dragons swept to and fro, while amongst them darted the small, bright poppy-red Mags. To either side of the entrance to the Dark Queen's cavern sat a stern guard dragon. Roughly four times the height of a human, these were nevertheless about half the size of their queen. They were a sickly yellow colour; their hides waxy, shaggy carpets of tiny leaf-like scales, matted like unkempt hair. From their wings hung rags of this material, looking like yellow cobweb curtains.

For a moment Jena considered asking one of the Bryos to give them a lift to the wall, but decided against it. They would only sneer at Jena's request, their slavish obedience to the will of the Dark Queen obliterating any trace of consideration that might once have nestled inside their heartless chests.

From the cavern entrance a narrow, precariously winding path meandered down to the foot of the mountain. From there they had perhaps a thirty-minute walk through the dragon fields to the wall. As they descended the slope a Ptero descended onto the ledge behind them, the wind from its wings cooling the back of Jena's neck. The dragon clutched a squirming calf in its taloned grasp. Food for the Dark Queen. She preferred her food to be alive when she ate it.

"I can't wait to get out of these damned coveralls," Jena cursed.

"You do smell a bit funky."

"Of course I do! Do you realise how hot it gets inside a dragon's mouth?"

"Well—"

"No. You don't. You weren't the one chosen for the signal honour of bathing in wyrm spit."

"Jena, I—"

"Oh no, it was decreed that you were lacking any skill other than standing about writing stuff down, so I suggest that you shut your damned mouth instead of flapping it about spouting things of which you know nothing."

The two walked in silence for a while.

"When does Lizzie leave for the Fringe?" asked Susi, softly, inferring the true reason for her friend's anger.

"She was fifteen yesterday. They're coming to get her in three days," Jena told her, looking downcast. "It's not right.

She's so young. By the Ancestors, I'd go with her myself but for James. He's only four, and I won't leave him an orphan. Look, I'm sorry I snapped at you. It's not your fault. This is not an easy time for me."

"I understand that. You're a good mother. I'd offer to have James, you know, but if..." Susi trailed off.

"If I never returned you wouldn't want to be stuck with him permanently? It's true, he can be a handful."

"Look on the bright side. Maybe Lizzie'll come back after her tour of duty. I heard of a boy—"

"No-one comes back," said Jena, sourly. "Have you ever seen anyone return from the Fringe, personally? With your own eyes? No, I thought not. It's always a friend of a friend. No one really ever returns. People invent such things to comfort themselves that they are not sending their children away to die fighting the Euks. The dragons are the cruel masters of humanity. Life should not be this way."

"Be careful, Jena," Susi warned, glancing nervously to the fields through which they walked. The field to their left was empty but for tiny fern-like plants just poking through the rich soil. To their right the plants were more advanced, small dragon shapes depending from sturdy moss-covered stems. A red Mag tending the infant Bryos was fortunately too far away to hear Jena's rebellious words.

"Careful, my arse. They enslave us to serve their needs, to provide them with food - sometimes to *be* food - and to die in huge numbers on the Fringe battling savage Euks to keep themselves safe from harm, and from having to get their precious wyrm-hands dirty. If only I had the courage to fight against this tyranny, I—"

"Your husband tried fighting. Your husband died fighting. The dragons are too powerful, and too well protected behind the wall for us ever to hold any hope of victory."

"And I am too frightened, like most," Jena admitted. The walk to the wall was helping her to regain her composure. "I am not a brave person, Susi. I could never actually be a hero."

They were nearing the wall now. The fields here were more mature. Mags flitted about, helping green Pteros, yellow Bryos and red Mags to free themselves from their stems. Once free, the new-grown dragons stumbled about for a short time, flapping their wings madly, getting used to their independent movement. Then they flew, still somewhat erratically, towards the mountain caves to find one in which to shelter and await their first orders. The two women approached the pale yellow Bryo that had been tasked with taking them home. It waited by the wall, tapping its claws impatiently against the rock on which it squatted. Jena looked back at the enormous bulk of the mountain that the dragons called home. From this distance she could see the vast number of caves that pocked its vast rocky side, from the foot all the way up to the snowy mists that shrouded its peak. Most of those caves housed several dragons. There must be thousands of the creatures all told. Even if all of the villagers rebelled and banded together, even if they were able to reach this eyrie, they would be hopelessly outnumbered and helplessly weak.

She sighed and joined Susi sitting astride the Bryo's soft mossy back. It flapped its great wings once, twice, then heaved into the air.

As they plunged over the rim of the plateau that the dragons called home Jena clung tightly to the mossy hide of the Bryo. Behind her Susi gasped. Jena's breath caught in her throat as she saw how impossibly high they were. She knew from growing up in the shadow of Dragonhome that it was a massive, towering rock, impossible to climb, but at this dizzying height the wall seemed absurdly high. The mountain at the centre of that plateau, riddled with the caves in which the dragons roosted, added yet more height to this massive upheaval of rock which jutted out of a seemingly endless plain.

Jena risked opening her eyes. She could barely make out where her village lay amongst the forest of ginkgo trees that covered the land below the immense table of granite. The Bryo arrowed headlong down the sheer drop, the ground below rising to meet them with alarming speed. This morning they had been carried up to the top by an elderly Ptero which had been content to take its time, rising in gentle circles. The Ptero had been almost chatty, enquiring about their visit to the world above. Jena had been fascinated by its skin, which was covered with feathery green fronds, delicately divided, and rolled into tight spirals here and there. She had toyed with small green curls and had thoroughly enjoyed the flight. She had even thanked the dragon when it had left them at the top of the wall.

This creature was entirely different, and seemed to take vicious pleasure in manoeuvring at speeds that caused its passengers no little discomfort. Jena felt her stomach flip, and struggled to keep her breakfast down. She heard Susi whimper as the dragon bottomed out of the vertical dive in a tight arc, and with furious backthrusts of its powerful ribboned wings landed in the centre of The Scorching, a roughly circular area of ground perhaps a hundred yards or so across.

In stark contrast to the rest of the plain, which was densely coated with gingkos as far as the horizon, the clearing was entirely devoid of trees. The packed earth was black and fused into a glass-like surface. Here and there a charred stump showed that once, a long time ago, trees had grown here. Myth told that in the time of the Ancestors people had risen up against their dragon overlords in a brief bid for freedom. The revolution had been short-lived. The dragons had summoned a mighty storm to dampen the passions of the rebels and then used their fearsome ability to spit streams of fire, creating a whirling inferno that had destroyed everything here; people, trees, houses - even the ability of the earth to sustain new life. The Scorching was a permanent reminder of the terrible power of the dragons, and served to quelled all thoughts of rebellion.

Jena slid from the Bryo's back and stood gingerly, her legs trembling. Susi fell to the ground and sat down, panting heavily, knuckles white and face drained of blood. The dragon curled its lip and raised its mossy wings to leave.

"Wait!" called Jena. "We are ordered to return tomorrow. Will you send a Ptero to carry us up the wall?"

The dragon snorted derision, and thrust upwards with its mighty back legs. The outstretched wings pulled at the air and the creature rose away from them leaving a warm rush of air.

"I'll take that as a yes," Jena said. She pulled Susi to her feet and the two walked home. Jena relaxed once they entered the trees. The Scorching was a bad place, full of bad feelings. They followed the path that wound its way between vast tree-trunks up to twenty-five feet in diameter. The trees rose majestically, some to as high as a hundred and fifty feet. Many were a thousand years old, it was said, and had been here long before the coming of the dragons. Even on the brightest of days the forest floor would have been depressingly gloomy but for the occasional light-windows that the forester Shambrook and her team of expert climbers made and maintained in the thick canopy high overhead.

As they reached edge of the village they were greeted with a loud bark as Bryan scampered to meet them, leaping up to express his joy on their return. Quite how the big yellow dog always knew that they were coming home was a mystery. Maybe he sensed the dragon landing half a mile away. Jena threw out her arms and hugged his wriggly fur. After Jena had made a fuss of him he gently took her hand and tugged her towards her house.

"It looks like he wants you back home," smiled Susi. "I'll be off, too. See you tomorrow, eh?" She angled off towards her own home as Bryan fell into step with Jena. Woman and dog walked the short distance to Jena's house. Home, like all of the other dwellings in the village, was three small rooms hollowed out of the trunk of a living gingko. Shambrook was an expert at carving living spaces into the vast trunks without killing the trees itself. Once she had hollowed out the desired shape, she coated the new walls with a potion of her own devising that not only healed the tree's wounds but also created a pleasant aroma and repelled insects. She had added Jena's third room shortly after James had been born.

As Jena approached the leather hanging that served as her front door it was flung wide and a breathless, wide-eyed Lizzie burst out.

"Mam!" she cried, obviously distressed, "Mam, James has… I was just playing tug with Bryan. And then James. I don't know! There's a man!"

"Whoa, take it easy," Jena tried to calm her daughter, taking her in her arms and giving her a reassuring hug. "Now start at the beginning. And tell me clearly what's wrong."

Lizzie took a deep breath and launched into rapid speech. "I was out here playing with Bryan and his tug-rope. James was asleep on the bed. When I got tired I went in to see if he was OK only he wasn't there. A man was, though, and he was sitting by the bed. I thought at first that he'd come to take me off to the Fringe a bit early, but he wanted you. He said James is safe, but I couldn't see him anywhere. And then I saw you and I ran out and, Mam, what's happening?"

"I don't know, but I'm damned well going to find out." She stormed inside, her mind wheeling with a combination of panic, anger and indignation.

As Lizzie had said, a man sat on the chair by the bed in the far corner of the room. He was perhaps forty years old, shaven-headed, and wore a long coat. His rangy legs stretched before him, high leather boots covering his feet which were crossed at the ankles.

"Ah, the dentist!" he said, in a low mocking tone.

"Where's my son?" Jena demanded.

"My name is Johnson Miller," the man said, ignoring her. Jena grabbed a knife from the shelf by the door and crossed to the man. She pointed the knife directly at his eye.

"Where is my son?" she spat. In one swift, fluid movement the man swept his legs against hers, knocking her off balance. He stood, grabbed her arm and wrenched it so that the knife clattered to the floor. Jena gasped as he twisted further causing flashes of pain to slice through her elbow.

"Leave my Mam alone!" Lizze yelled. Bryan launched himself at the man with a fearsome snarl, but was kicked backwards before he could do any damage. He stood warily not far away, alternately growling and whimpering. The man towered over Jena, scowling down at her.

"What a violent family you do have, dentist," he growled. "I suggest that you keep them quiet while I tell you what I want. Otherwise, I might just take it into my head to kill your cur and defile your daughter. Now sit, and be silent!" He threw Jena down into a chair and moved nearer the door, cutting off Lizzie's escape. Jena rubbed at her arm and eyed the man. Bryan rested his heavy head on her knee, trying to comfort her. Her mind was a vortex of twisting emotion.

"Your son is alive," growled the interloper, "at least for now. He will remain safe until you have completed a little job for us, at which point we will return him to you unharmed. If you fail us in this enterprise, then you will never see him again. At least, not all of him. Now, have I impressed upon you how serious your situation is?"

Jena nodded, tight-lipped.

"Good. I think that once you hear them, you will agree with our aims, if not our methods. Now, you are one of the privileged few who been granted access to Dragonhome on a regular basis. On your next visit, I want you to take this with you." He hoisted a leather satchel from the floor and slung the strap over his shoulder. "It contains a number of these," he continued, reaching into the bag and taking out a stoppered glass flask with a curiously shaped neck that resembled the sinuous throat of a dragon. He handed the flask to Jena. It contained a black, oily liquid. As she turned the glass, the viscous contents clung to the sides as if reluctant to obey the demands of gravity. She checked the cork stopper. It held secure but could easily be released with a twist. She briefly considered throwing the contents in the man's face and while he was blinded thrusting the knife from the floor into his black heart, but the thought of what might happen to James stayed her hand.

"What do you actually want?" she asked.

"When you are next up there, on the plateau, you are to take a pleasant walk among the dragon fields. At each field you pass, you will pour a measure of this liquid into the soil. The neck of the flask is so designed as to dispense the required amount."

"And this will do what?"

"It will poison the fields. It will blacken the stems and destroy the roots of the dragonyoung plants. It will prevent the wyrms from reproducing. It will signal the end of their dominion over us as they all age and die. It will herald the beginning of freedom for humankind. Tell me that's not a laudable aim."

"I'm all for freedom, but at what expense? Slaughtering the dragon's babies?"

"They aren't babies. They're plants, weeds, a blight on us all. We've finally managed to obtain an effective weedkiller, and you're going to be our deliverer, in more ways than one."

"And if I'm caught?"

"The wyrms will likely kill and eat you. Hell, they'll probably do that anyway once they find out that you're the one who poisoned them. It won't take them long. Frankly, we don't care if you die, as long as you get the job done. Neither should you, for that matter. Consider yourself already dead; what you have to think about now is the life of your son."

"You bastard."

"So I've been told. When do you next visit Dragonhome?"

Jena briefly considered lying, but realised that it would do little good. Johnson Miller no doubt had spies watching her movements. "Tomorrow," she said.

"So soon? Excellent. Then I shall return in two days for your report. If everything goes according to plan then your son will be returned to you. Entertain no thoughts of going against me. I will not hesitate to kill your boy."

He strode out of the house, leaving the shoulder-bag on the floor. Jena considered her options. She could simply pretend that she had poisoned the dragons, but eventually it would become obvious that she hadn't and Johnson Miller seemed to be a man who would exact vicious revenge. She could warn the dragons, but that would not help her to get James back. She could only see one course of action.

Bryan licked her hand with his smooth, wet tongue and Lizzie hugged her neck.

"Mam?" she asked, "What will you do?"

"I think I have to poison the dragon fields."

The next morning she and Susi waited at The Scorching for a dragon to come and lift them to Dragonhome. Jena had told Susi all about her visitor of the previous evening, the kidnapping of James, and what she had to do. She had urged Susi not to come, but her friend had insisted on accompanying her. It would look odd for her to go alone, Susi argued, and might raise the dragons' suspicions.

A sound from above announced the arrival of a dragon, which fell to earth gently in the centre of the charred clearing. Jena was relieved when she recognised the old Ptero that had taken them up the day before. The dragon nodded in acknowledgement as Jena and Susi crossed over to it.

"Good day," it breathed, its voice almost a purr.

"Hello again," said Jena. The flasks in her shoulder bag clinked as she climbed onto the dragon's broad back and she spoke quickly in an attempt to cover the sound. "I'm pleased that you will be taking us up. The Bryo that carried us down yesterday seemed determined to break our necks."

"I apologise. The Bryos do tend to be a little careless, I am afraid. In addition, I imagine that it resented being forced to interact with hominids and took its frustration out on you."

"Don't you resent us?"

"On the contrary, I have always rather liked your species, what few I have met. I maintain, and long have, that we dragons need not treat you as if you were ours to do with as we pleased, as mere minions. There should be more give and take between our species, more consideration. I am not alone in this opinion. My friends and I believe that we all could live in harmony, to the betterment of all, but we must obey the Dark Queen. She has the strength to bend us all to her will."

"That's very interesting. Do you mind if I know your name? I am Jena, and this woman frowning furiously at me is Susi."

"What are you doing?" hissed Susi. "Don't talk to it. It might take it into its head to eat us or burn us to cinders."

There was an odd huffing grating sound, which Jena realised was coming from the Ptero. The dragon was laughing.

"We are not all martinets," it said gruffly. "I, for instance, make it a rule never to eat anything with which I can hold a conversation. And my name is Luedtke. I will be your pilot today. Please prepare for take-off." He arced his wings and they rose gently from the ground.

"Luedtke, would you mind answering a question?"

"Not at all, hominid Jena. The more we learn about each other the more pleasant will our lives be."

"OK. You have no gender, right? No male-female divide?"

"That is correct. This is much simpler than your own arrangements, which seem to me to be unnecessarily complicated. For one thing, it takes two of you to make a new hominid. Inefficient. In addition you appear to choose your clothing and face-paint based entirely upon the shape of your genitals. This strikes me as hilariously pointless."

"Actually, I agree with you there. But here's my question: how come, if you are truly androgynous, you have a Queen? Why not a Monarch, or simply Leader - a title with no gender implication?"

"Ah, that is pure affectation on Daf'q's part. She romances that it sounds impressive. Typical Pino behaviour."

"How did Daf'q get to be in charge?"

"Well, she's the Pino."

"Sorry, I don't understand."

"Very well. How much do you know of dragon society?"

"Just what I've seen. You are grown in fields, there are different kinds of dragon, you sometimes eat people—"

"Or burn us alive with incandescent flame from your mouths," added Susi, uncomfortable with her friend's conversation with the dragon. Jena, on the other hand, was fascinated. Not only was she learning new things, the talk was helping to distract her from worry about James, and from what she must do once they were up on the plateau.

"Shall I let you in on a secret?" asked Luedtke, and continued without waiting for a response. "We cannot actually breathe fire. That is just a story, one of many, put about by the Bryos to keep you hominids in check. We do not excrete coal from our rear ends, either."

"I hadn't heard that one," admitted Jena.

"Oh. Then perhaps the propaganda begins to lose its hold. But rest assured, hominid Susi, we cannot burn you."

"I thought that The Scorching was created by an angry dragon's fire?"

"The burned, flattened area where we met? Happenstance, only. Certainly the fabled battle took place as stated, in a storm. Lightning struck and devastated the area just as the dragons attacked. We claimed that it was our doing, of course, to frighten the hominids into submission. It has become a useful threat to hold over your heads, but an empty one in reality. We can no more breathe fire than you can. What we can do, however, is to rip out your insides with our claws, or hold you down while we pluck off your limbs. I would rather not, to be honest, but we do have that strength."

"Don't trust it," said Susi. "It's a trap of some sort."

"If this were true we would have known years ago," said Jena. "Why are you telling us this now?"

"No hominid has ever taken the trouble to speak to me before. Mostly they just quiver at the sight of us. One man cried, I remember."

"The reputation of the dragons is fearsome, that's true. Most people are terrified, but the few who are given access to Dragonhome, like us, must become more comfortable and converse with you."

"Not really. You are the first to talk to me for, well, ever. It is quite refreshing."

"I agree. But please carry on. You were telling us about Daf'q?"

"Was I? Ah yes, my apologies. I tend to drift off the point these days. It comes to us all with age, I am afraid. So, the reason Daf'q is our ruler… well, you know that we dragons are of five families?"

"You are? I hadn't counted."

"Yes. For instance, I am of the Pteridophyta. An unimaginably long time ago, hominids found a way to grow winged creatures from five separate fauna divisions. In my family's case, the ferns. We are Fern Dragons."

"Wait. *People* created dragons?"

"Indeed. You did not know this? I imagine the idea was to create a new beast of burden that would perform a lot of fetching and carrying, or perhaps to make steeds swifter than any you had. We dragons didn't like that idea and turned the tables, instead making you serve us, tend to our needs, keep animals to provide us with food." Luedtke snorted. "Look after our teeth. You know, it has always seemed odd to me that a race that has been subject to persecution and slavery as we were should want to inflict those very things on others."

"People created dragons?"

"Yes, and they lived to regret it. To continue, in addition to we Pteros, there are the Bryophyta - the Moss Dragons, the Magnoliophyta - Flower Dragons, and the Pinophyta - Pine Dragons."

"Pteros, Bryos, Mags and Pines, got it."

"Yes. Ferns, mosses and flowers are grown in the fields, but the pines are different. There exists but one of these, far larger than any other, and she rules all. When her death approaches, or when she reaches a certain age, she shakes scores of seeds from beneath her wings, which begin to grow. Eventually she devours all of her children but the strongest, which she raises to adulthood. When the younger is ready, she kills her mother and assumes the throne. Daf'q slaughtered her parent five years ago."

"Charming. Wait - that's only four. You said there were five families."

"Ah yes, the Eukaryota - grey, slimy Fungus Dragons. They are wild & unpredictable creatures, violent and cruel, controlled by no-one. They exist beyond the fringes of the kingdom. Sadly, as you know only too well, Daf'q sees fit to send hordes of your kin to fight them out there and lose their lives. She fears that without such cannon-fodder to keep them busy the Euks will come and attack us here."

"My daughter goes to that fight shortly."

"Then you have my sympathy. I regret that I am unable to offer any comfort that your daughter's death will have any meaning. My belief is that the Euks are quite happy where they are, and not in the least bothered about us here. It is nothing more than senseless slaughter to send hominids to die under their claws. Ah, we are here."

Luedtke set them down at the top of the precipice and bid them a cheery farewell. It fell to exercising its wings as they walked away, easing its old joints. After her conversation with the old Fern Dragon, Jena had even more doubts what she had to do. Plainly, all dragonkind were not evil. There existed at least one, and likely more, that had kind hearts and a more accepting view of humanity than they had been led to believe. If she poisoned them all, she would be killing innocents as well as evil tyrants. Now that she thought about it, perhaps all of the dragon young were innocents.

Perhaps their enslavement of humankind was learned behaviour; learned from the evil Pine Dragon that ruled them. If only there existed some way of pruning the Pines from the dragon family tree then both races might live in harmony.

It was a pipedream, but a lovely thought. In reality she had no choice. Yes, Jena hated what she had to do, but she would do it. For James' sake.

"Come on," she intoned, "Let's get on with this."

Jena took one of the swan-necked flasks from her bag as they walked the path between two fields. To their right grew ranks of almost ripe Bryos, while on their left a swathe of young plants carried buds that had not yet formed enough for Jena to make out what kind of dragon they might be. From the pinkish tint of the stems she might hazard a guess that they were Mags. She unstoppered the flask and hesitated, sighing.

"Hurry up," Susi urged, "None can see. Let's just kill the evil sods, clean the queen's teeth, and get out of here as soon as we can."

"It's not that simple. They're not all evil. Luedtke was friendly, even sympathetic."

"They *are* all evil because even if they disagree with treating people as slaves they do nothing to stop it. And I can't believe you're hesitating when your son's life is at stake. Let me do it, if you won't."

"You're right, of course. I have to do this for James." She tipped the flask and a gobbet of oily fluid fell from the flask. It soaked remarkably quickly into the soil. She repeated the action on the other side of the path and they quickly walked on.

"What about those fields over there?" Susi pointed out other fields beyond those adjacent to the path. There were no paths to these further fields. Dragons had no use for paths since they could fly. The trail of hard, packed earth that they walked on was maintained purely for the use of humans that were summoned to Dragonhome, although why they couldn't simply be flown directly to the mountain rather than having to traipse from the cliff-edge was beyond Jena. The women edged their way between the already spoiled Bryo field on their right and a field of young Pteros that adjoined it. Jena poured a measure of the poison into the rich earth of this field also, emptying her first flask. Three fields down, perhaps a dozen to go.

"Hominid! What is it you do there?" Jena whipped about, momentarily surprised to see nothing before realising that she was thinking in two dimensions. She looked up to see a small Mag, perhaps eight feet from head to tail, hovering close enough that she could make out the individual petals that covered its skin. It wore an expression of such concern, apprehension and hurt that Jena immediately felt remorse for her actions.

Susi took a step forward. "Just exploring," she said. "Nothing to worry about."

"Oh, but I do worry, hominid. You poured blackness into the soil of my young. What is your purpose?"

"That was merely—"

"Poison. It was poison," Jena interrupted her friend. "I'm sorry, Susi, I can't do this. There must be another way, other than lying and destroying innocents. Will you listen to my explanation, dragon, before taking action? Please?"

"You are Jena, the dentist?"

"I am. You know my name?"

"Luedtke sent me to speak with you. He said that you might be the one for whom we have long been waiting."

"I don't understand."

"Nor will you, unless you justify to me your actions here in slaughtering the innocent young. Then I shall decide whether to explain further, or whether to simply eviscerate you where you stand. Choose your words carefully." The Mag settled to the ground on its powerful hind legs and sat back using its tail as support. It was easily within striking distance, which made Jena's voice tremble slightly as she began her story. Her voice steadied as her tale went on, and the Mag began to show interest. She told it of their nerve-wracking descent the previous day, and of arriving home to find her son gone. She told of Johnson Miller and his threat to kill her son if she did not do as he asked. She made clear her strong belief that he meant every word that he had said. She showed the Mag the flasks of the dark Weedkiller, and explained its foul purpose; that it was designed to wipe out the dragon species, at her hand.

"Then you were doing this to save your offspring?" the Mag asked. Jena nodded. "You must understand then, that if I end your life now it is for the same reason?" Again Jena indicated her understanding, and tensed in preparation for the killer blow.

"I believe, however, that there is a better solution for both of us," the Mag said. "I think that we can help each other. You may call me Thibodeau. Luedtke tells me that you believe—"

"How? We've only just left him. There's been no time."

"We do not only speak with words."

"You're telepathic?"

"No we are not. We have developed a way of speaking at a distance by use of many subtle wing positions. As you left it, Luedtke told me that you believe as we do, that our two species should live in harmony and mutual respect."

"Who is 'we'?"

"Certainly almost all of my family, and most of Luedtke's. Perhaps not the Bryos, but they are followers in nature and will ride with the prevailing wind. If we can remove the Pinophyte line and its control over the Bryos, then we will all be able to work together to make this a fairer world for everyone, whether dragon or hominid."

"Then overpower Daf'q and get rid of her. There must easily be enough of you."

"She would see us coming, or her guards would, and she would order all of the Bryos to defend the entrance to her cavern. There would result a huge battle with much loss of life, even before we could reach her. A better way would be for us to approach her from behind, unseen, for a surprise attack. Luckily, there does exist a rear entrance to her cavern. It is small, but a Mag, or several, might squeeze through unseen and kill Daf'q while she sleeps. There is just one problem, which is where you come in."

"I'm not sure I'm going to like this."

"The rear entrance was created by hominids at some forgotten time, which is presumably why it is so small. It was also barred by them and locked from the inside. We once attempted to break through the barrier, an action for which a dozen Mags were slaughtered. You, hominid, have access to Daf'q's cavern. You are also a hominid, and therefore it is likely that you would know how to open the barrier. After you next treat Daf'q, we want you sneak to the rear of her cavern and let us in. We will do the rest. Will you do this thing for us? For us all?"

"No. I will not risk my son's life."

"Then we shall make sure that he is safe first. We will rescue your offspring and then you will help us. Do we have an accord?"

"I don't even know where James is."

"We can find him. We have had a friend watching you for some weeks, since you first came to our attention as one who might be sympathetic to our aims. This friend saw the tall hominid and his cohorts remove your offspring, and, I believe, has the ability to discover his whereabouts. We can go and fetch him now, if you wish?"

"Dragon, if you rescue my son, then I will lend what little aid I can to your cause."

"Very well. I have to say, this has been a good conversation. Climb upon my back. I am unable to bear two of you, so you must stay here, friend of Jena."

"Jena, are you sure about this?" Susi asked her friend.

"I'm not sure of anything," Jena replied, settling herself onto Thibodeau's back. The scales that covered its torso were shaped like butterfly wings, like the leaves of the ginkgo. She tucked her legs in behind the dragon's wings. "I'm just riding the wind, Susi, and this particular wind promises to bring my son safely home." Susi shrugged and sat cross-legged on the ground and leaned against the backpack containing the dental equipment.

"We shall return once the young hominid is safe, Jena-friend, and you will both continue to your appointment with the Dark Queen and change the world's axis." The Flower Dragon took off, angling back towards the edge of the plateau.

They swung down the precipice, in rather less frenetic a manner than the Bryo had descended the previous day. Jena's mind was surprisingly calm, in view of the myriad things it had to process. Could she trust these dragons? Who was the dragons' friend, their spy? Would attempting to rescue James actually put her son in danger? Perhaps he was already in constant danger, wherever he was. She briefly considered all these things, only to dismiss them without trying to answer. It was easier to act that way. She was indeed riding the wind wherever it took her, and for some unknown reason she found herself trusting this creature that rode the wind with her.

As they landed close to the edge of The Scorching, Bryan scampered up to them as usual. Jena slid from Thibodeau's back and threw out her arms to greet the dog. This time, however, he ignored her and sat before the red dragon. The dragon yipped, then barked. Bryan emitted a curious rising whine, and the dragon barked once more. The dog huffed, then stood and came to greet Jena, wagging his big tail.

Jena eyed Thibodeau curiously. "What was that? Were you talking to my dog?"

"I was indeed communicating with your canine. Such communication is comprised of both vocal elements and body language. You do not do this?"

"Well, I say 'Who's a good boy?' occasionally."

"Then you miss much. The canine does certainly believe that he may find your son, were you only to allow him to bury his nose in one of your offspring's garments for a moment, as a reminder of his scent."

"Bryan? Bryan's your spy?" The dog barked. Jena took a moment, then spoke again. "Then let's go to my house. Will you fit through the trees?"

"I am sufficiently flexible," Thibodeau nodded, and folded its wings tightly against its body, like a flower closing up for the night.

"Heel, Bryan," commanded Jena, and the ragtag trio made their way through the forest towards Jena's tree. Most villagers that saw them simply stood and stared at the unique sight of a dragon walking through the forest. None spoke. This may have been from fear, or possibly amazement that a dragon could be small enough to walk beneath the trees. Mags rarely descended from the plateau. The path was occasionally a tight squeeze for Thibodeau, but the dragon was lithe and flexible enough to find a way through.

When they reached home Jena greeted a worried Lizzie warmly, and reassured her that her early return was nothing to worry about. When she stepped outside to be introduced to the dragon she simply gaped.

"It is a friend," Jena told her daughter, "Thibodeau is going to help us find James, and then maybe begin a series of events that would lead to your not having to go to the Fringe."

"Is it a 'he' or a 'she'?" Lizzie asked, standing close to her mother.

"I am neither, offspring of Jena," Thibodeau said, "I am simply me. I believe that it is customary for hominids to greet a new friend by the shaking of hands?" The dragon extended a foreleg, the attached wing unfurling gracefully. Lizzie hesitantly took one of the large claws and shook gently. Her eyes gleamed. "Now, if you could please provide canine Bryan with an article of the clothing of your brother, then we shall quickly rescue him."

Lizzie ran to into the house for a moment before emerging clutching a large cloth, which she held out to the dragon. Thibodeau inclined his head, indicating the patient dog. Lizzie took the cloth to Bryan, who buried his nose in the material, snuffling loudly. He circled the area in front of the house for a moment, sniffing the ground, then circled Jena's tree. Three-quarters of the way round he gave a satisfied bark, and headed off down a rarely-used path.

"Follow the canine," Thibodeau told Jena, "I am unable to move as swiftly between the trees as you, but I will be close behind."

"Lizzie, wait here!" Jena told her daughter, then hastened after Bryan. Lizzie watched the red dragon stoop beneath a low branch as it followed more slowly, disappearing into the trees. Lizzie looked about the now empty space doubtfully.

"The hell with it," she said, and sprinted after them.

Bryan led Jena out of the village along a meandering path to a part of the forest that she did not know. The path twisted, forked and turned, but generally led them east. After some fifteen minutes Bryan stopped, sat, and look back as Jena caught up.

"What's wrong, boy?" She peered through the undergrowth and saw a most unusual structure. It was built, rather than carved from the trees, and it was made of metal. Huge sheets of the stuff, far more than Jena had ever seen in her life before. The few metal items in the village, pots and pans mostly, and a few knives, were brought to them by the trade caravan that made the hazardous journey from the south once a year to trade for medicines that the villagers made from the ginkgo. Jena's dental instruments had come to her father that way, and they had passed to her when he died.

Stained metal walls supported a corrugated roof which was covered with moss and debris that had fallen from nearby trees. There were no visible windows, but a path had been worn to a door set in the centre of the facing wall. A faded sign above the door could just be read through decades of accumulated grime. It said 'PROJECT 217 - NURSERY 3'.

Bryan whined, and took a step forward.

"Wait," Jena commanded. Without the backup of a dragon ally she was not at all confident about a confrontation with the imposing Johnson Miller and an unknown number of cohorts. She laid a reassuring hand on Bryan's warm head and looked into his eyes. "Good boy," she whispered. "Let's wait for your dragon friend." He licked her hand, wet and warm.

She looked back up and her heart skipped a beat. Lizzie! What was she doing there? Her daughter was by the right corner of the building. Jena frantically waved to draw Lizzie's attention, but the girl's attention was fixed on the weird metal building and she crossed towards the door. Jena stood, but the door opened before she could move to warn her daughter. Johnson Miller stepped out right in front of Lizzie, who jumped with a small squeal. For a tall man he was exceptionally quick, both of wit and limb. He grabbed Lizzie's shoulders and spun her round in front of him so that both captor and captive faced the trees. His left arm held her tight against him, while his right held a dagger pointed at Lizzie's neck.

"Well now," he said loudly. "I never thought you'd have it in you, dentist. I assume you are out there, watching? I doubt that your daughter would have wandered out here of her own accord."

Jena remained silent. Bryan shifted impatiently, but continued to obey the command to wait.

"Ah well, it's up to you. Skulk there and watch me slaughter your daughter if you must. Or perhaps I shall have a little fun first." He moved his left hand slowly across Lizzie's chest, lifting and pinching. She gasped and tears rimmed her eyes. This was too much.

"Let her go!" said Jena, stepping out of the bushes. "She's innocent, leave her and my son out of this."

"I'm very disappointed in you. You should just have done what I asked. Now you'll all die, as an example to our next unwilling volunteer."

"Listen, believe it or not," Jena tried, "We're on the same side. We both want an end to the dragons' dominance over us."

"Then why did you not kill them all as I asked?"

"Because they are not all evil. Many are good, and want the same as us."

"What the hell gave you that idea?"

"I have friends, dragon friends. They are ready to overthrow their ruler, with my help. We can trust them, help them, and win our freedom without slaughtering scores of innocents."

"You idiot. You think you can trust them? You can never trust a wyrm. The people who grew them here knew that, right from the start! Where do you think I got the Weedkiller? Wyrms are slimy, black-hearted evil. There's not a one of them that isn't a blight on this land. The only good dragon is a dead—"

Lizzie stamped her heel down hard on Johnson Miller's instep, at the same time elbowing him in the belly and wrenching herself away. He grimaced in agony, doubling over and dropping the knife.

"Purple!" he yelled, presumably to people inside the building. "Fuller! Kill the—" A large patch of red blurred above Jena's head as she hugged Lizzie safely to her. The arc of Thibodeau's leap brought it crashing down on Johnson Miller before he could finish his command. The dragon's talons ended his life before he even knew what was happening. Bryan could restrain himself no longer and, barking loudly, ran to the dragon's side. He grabbed the dead man's foot and shook it savagely, then sat by Thibodeau with a satisfied expression on his furry face.

"Lizzie, are you alright?" Jena looked her daughter in the eyes and knew at once that she was. "Well done, daughter."

"Don't sound so surprised, Mam. I am going off to fight in a few days." She glanced at Johnson's Miller's body with a look of satisfaction. "Serve him right, the creepy groper."

"Hominids inside!" called Thibodeau, in a deep portentous tone that Jena had not heard before. "Your leader is dead. Bring out the boy unharmed, and we will allow you your pathetic lives!"

"What's with the voice?" asked Jena as she moved to stand by the dragon.

"If used sparingly, on such occasions as this, fear can be a useful tool. I intended my tone to make those inside nervous. Did my voice not inspire fear, hominid Jena?"

"I guess. Did you have to kill him?" she asked, looking down at the corpse.

"I believe that I did. He was about to give the order to have your son killed."

"Well, thank you," she said, resting her hand on Thibodeau's haunch.

The door opened, and two women emerged, blinking in the light. Between them was James, tear-tracks running down his filthy face. He ran to Jena with a cry of "Mam!" and she swung him around into a loving hug. He clung to her neck, sniffing.

"Hominids!" Thibodeau commanded the two women, using its 'scary' voice once more. "Do you have anything to say?"

"It was all him!" the one dressed in purple jabbered. The other nodded, and added "He made us do it!"

"Then think on this, puny hominids." Jena raised an eyebrow, but Thibodeau was obviously enjoying itself. "You may go, but always remember that we know where you live. I know your appearance, and I know your stink. Should either of you ever come to my attention again I will find you and I will burn you. I will turn you to ash from the inside out with my dragonfire!"

"I thought you said—" whispered Jena. Thibodeau nudged her hard with its wing, and she took the hint to remain silent.

"Open a little wider please," Jena said, moistening the brush once more. Dark Queen Daf'q complied, allowing Jena to scrub the far side of the rearmost molar. In the mirror she saw the tartar fall away under the stiff bristles to leave the tooth free of gunk.

"There," she said, "All done!" Susi took the brush and the mirror first, followed by a bucket full of pieces of rotting flesh. then helped Jena to climb out over the sharp teeth. "You should drink, your majesty, to thoroughly clean the mouth of particles, but your teeth are now as clean as I can make them."

"Finally," Daf'q declaimed. "You took far too long. Leave now." The enormous Pinophyte settled her head upon her folded front legs and closed her eyes. She began to snore, a surprisingly small sound from so huge a creature.

"Right, come on," hissed Jena.

"Are you sure?" asked Susi, "I still don't trust them."

"I made a deal. Let's find this back door and get it open. Thibodeau and its friends will be waiting." She walked around the edge of the enormous cavern, skirting the sleeping bulk of the dragon queen. The light grew dim; any illumination that might have reached this far back into the cavern was blocked by its inhabitant. Jena did manage to find a small entrance, however, by dint of noticing an area of wall that was slightly darker than the rest. Both man and Mag sized, it gave onto a short passage. They entered, and Jena pushed a sharp stick into the translucent flask that she had brought with her. This pierced a seal within the container that separated two liquids which when combined reacted to produce light. Shambrook, who had provided the flask, called this process chemiluminescence, but Jena failed to understand why she might ever need to know this. It was enough for her that it worked.

The flask cast an eerie green glow, enough to light their way. Their way proved no more than a few yards, however, before they reached a metal doorway set into the wall. It was, as expected, locked. On the wall next to the door was a small panel holding a grid of buttons which bore different numbers. Pushing the buttons achieved nothing - the panel was dusty, dirty and dead.

"Here," said Susi from behind her, and pulled a lever that Jena had not spotted. The panel of numbers lit up. Presumably, she had to press the correct sequence of numbers to open the door, but what sequence? She tried 1-2-3-4, to no avail.

"Try it backwards," Susi suggested. 4-3-2-1 failed too. This could take forever. Perhaps if she cleaned a little more dirt off... yes. There were letters, too, three or four per button. She tried D-F-Q. No.

D-R-A-G-O-N also failed, as did P-I-N-O, B-R-Y-O, P-T-E-R-O and M-A-G. She mashed her fist against all the buttons at once in frustration, but again, there was no response. What could the code be? The door had obviously been put in here long ago, perhaps when the dragons were first moved onto the plateau.

"Project 217," Jena muttered. She held her breath and pushed the three numbers. There was a click, and the door swung inward allowing in a flood of light. Thibodeau stood outside on a narrow ledge. Beyond and below the dragon Jena saw water, a glittering ocean that stretched as far as the eye could see. She was amazed. How come none of the villagers knew that this vast sea was so close, on the opposite side of the plateau?

That was a question for later. She stood aside to allow Thibodeau access, and the dragon stooped to enter. "You have my admiration, Jena," it said. "Now leave us to our task. Wait in this spot. It will be very dangerous to be in the Dark Queen's cavern." Three other Mags filed behind Thibodeau into the passageway.

"Is that all of you?" Jena asked. "She's awfully big for just four of you to handle."

"We know her weak spots," Thibodeau answered, "and the Pteros are mounting an assault from the front shortly. Luedtke witnessed that you managed to open this door and has flown over the mountain to co-ordinate the Ptero attack. Idris," Thibodeau spoke to the Mag immediately behind it, "you will attack her belly. I shall attack her eyes. Becca-ree, you back me up. If I fall, keep attacking her eyes. They are her weakest spot. Chorlton, you attack wherever you spot a weakness. Keep her busy until the Pteros break through. Courage, my friends. We shall prevail."

The four Mags squeezed through the dark passageway. Despite Thibodeau's warning, and Susi's frantic hissing of her name, Jena went after them. As she followed Chorlton's tail down the passage it occurred to her that we was doing exactly the same thing that Lizzie had done earlier. Was she putting herself in danger in the same way? If so, it could not be helped. She simply had to witness what was about to happen. The next few minutes could change the world. She stood just inside the passage entrance as the four Mags positioned themselves around the dozing Pinophyte. After a few moments Susi joined her.

Thibodeau glanced at its companions. Receiving three nods, it leaped high into the air, extended its claws and crashed down onto Daf'q's head, sinking those thorny claws deep beneath her woody skin. At the same time Idris raked its rear feet down Daf'q's belly, close to the rear leg, dislodging wooded scales that scattered across the floor. Becca-ree and Chorlton tore at the Queen's wings.

The Dark Queen roared her pain as she leaped to her feet and stretched her mighty wings high. Chorlton was caught between wing and cavern roof and died immediately, crushed against the hard rock. Becca-ree rolled sideways out of the way, then took to the air, looking for a new place to attack the writhing body beneath. Thibodeau added its teeth to its claw attack, ripping a hole close by Daf'q's eye. The Dark Queen shook her head violently, dislodgiung Thibodeau and throwing it against the cavern wall. She twisted her neck and gabbed Idris in her mighty jaws, taking off the Mag's head with one clean bite. Daf'q roared her fury, dark gore dripping from her jaws.

Things were going badly. Outside the cavern mouth Jena could see only rapidly moving shadows as Luedtke's Pteros fought with the Bryo guards. She fervently hoped that the battle outside was going better than this one, and that soon the aged Fern Dragon would be able to reinforce the two small Mags that remained inside. Thibodeau staggered to its feet, swaying woozily.

"You dare!" hissed the huge Pine Dragon. "You pathetic fools. I will slaughter all of your kin for this. But first, you die slowly."

Becca-ree swooped towards Daf'q's glittering multi-faceted eyes, claws extended, but the Dark Queen batted the Mag aside easily. Becca-ree fell motionless to the floor. This whole plan had been a serious mistake. The Mags were no match for the awesome power of the Pine Dragon. She was every inch of her a queen, dark and mighty. She glowered down now at Thibodeau, sneering her contempt.

"You, it was," she snarled. "You led this revolt."

"Indeed," Thibodeau growled, inching sideways, still looking for an opportunity to attack. Daf'q shot out a limb, her leathery wing sending a gust of air that lifted Jena's hair as it passed. She grabbed Thibodeau around the middle and flung the Mag down on its back, helpless.

"Know then," she taunted, "That you will die slowly, in agony, as I tear off your limbs one by one. Perhaps then you might appreciate the glory of your Queen!" She tightened her grip, and the tips of her claws pierced Thibodeau's skin, causing the Mag to cry out in pain.

"Now, where shall I start?" said Daf'q, and with her other forefoot pointed to each of Thoibodeau's limbs in turn. She coughed, then recited "Eeny, meeny, miny, mo. Ah, say good bye to your left leg, you…" She coughed again, and frowned.

"Just kill me and finish it," Thibodeau gasped. Daf'q swayed, and shook her head.

"What… what have you done?" she breathed, releasing the Mag and staggering sideways. A few scales fell from her neck. Thibodeau rolled onto its side and stared at the Dark Queen. At the far side of the cavern Becca-ree lifted its head. Dark Queen Daf'q's legs gave way and she crashed to the ground.

"It hurts!" she wailed. "What have you done, Mag?"

"This was not my doing, Daf'q," Thibodeau frowned.

"No, it was mine!" Jena strode into the cavern to stand by Thibodeau.

"What could… what could a pathetic hominid do?" hissed Daf'q, her face twisted with pain. Scales fell in scores from her heaving torso.

"Me? Not much," said Jena, "Except to coat your teeth with Weedkiller." Jena held up a flask of the dark liquid. The Dark Queen gasped and collapsed heavily to the ground as the life finally left her body. Luedtke rushed into the cavern entrance, saw the body of the Pinophyte, and relaxed with a dragon smile.

"Well done, my friend Jena," said Thibodeau, rising to its feet. "Well done indeed."

"I thought it wouldn't hurt to have a backup plan, just in case. So what happens now?"

"Well, for starters," said Thibodeau, curling a lip, "I think I broke a tooth. Do you think you could take a look?"

CLAUSTROPHOBIA

The first of four short Christmas-themed stories, this one was written for 'Tales by the Tree', a 'holiday' anthology from J.A.Mes Press.

Oh bum. How the jingle bells did this happen? Bloody centuries I've been doing this; how come all of a sudden I get stuck? I mean, yeah, in this dark I can see the sum total of sod all, but that's never stopped me before, even in really tight squeezes. The old Santa Wriggle usually gets me through any gap, as well as pleasing the elves at the Boxing Day Hullabaloo. Heh, it's all in the hips, you know.

It's become quite the dance at the party – great lines of elves and fairies, not to mention the missus, all doing the old Santa Wriggle. OK, yes, I call our celebration the Boxing Day Hullabaloo, and that's a British thing and I'm originally Dutch, but I just like that name, you know? Boxing Day – the day after Christmas according to the Brits. It trips off the tongue, don't you think? The Boxing Day Hullabaloo. Mind you, that won't be happening this year if I can't move myself.

The old Santa Wriggle is not doing it; not this sodding time. I can't shift, neither up nor down. I blame the missus' new mince pie recipe; the one with extra butter. I ate fifty yesterday. Might have gained a few inches, I suppose.

Bloody hell, it's pitch-black, my nose is pressed against filthy rotting bricks, I've got soot up my nose and I do *not* like it. I feel pressed in, squished tight. I might never get out, and then what? No more toys for good little girls and boys, no more coal for the naughty sods. It'll be a bloody disaster.

What's that, you say? Santa shouldn't swear? Piss off; you'd be letting out a non-stop stream of all the swears you know if you had to go through what I do once a year. Up and down all those sodding chimneys, and all within twenty-four hours? It's not bloody easy! Yes, yes, my time-slowing ability thingy helps, and that teleportation device that Elf

Ansafety came up with proved invaluable when people started living places without chimneys. But you know, that's not the whole job, not by a long chalk.

Have you ever thought what happens when a reindeer decides to have a poo right up there on someone's roof? Of course you haven't, your minds are all full of tinsel and glitter at Christmas. Well let me tell you, you can't just leave it up there, it'd stink for days. And imagine the questions once it was found. Nope, Muggins here has to shovel it all up and put it in the poo sack. Think yourselves lucky I don't get *that* mixed up with the sack of toys. Ah well, at least the reindeer don't drop their '*doings*' in flight, cos that'd be a terrible Christmas present for anyone down below.

This isn't getting me shifted, is it? I feel all closed in, trapped, and I'm sure there's not enough air in here. And what the hell's that sharp thing sticking into my bloody arse? Come on, Nick, see if you can reach round to have a feel. Ah, loose brick. Maybe if I can wiggle it out... OUCH! No no, bad idea, bad idea. Better leave it. No one wants a sharp brick corner poking them up *there*. I'd better see if I can call that lazy cow of a fairy down here, see if she has any bright ideas. Maybe she can magic me free.

OI! NUFF, WHERE ARE YOU? GET DOWN HERE!

Bet she's sitting on Dasher's antlers having a right old gossip. What's the use of having a fairy PA if all she does is sit about swapping recipes and talking about soap operas with reindeer?

I bet my beard's as black as, well, soot by now. I probably look more like Brian Blessed than Sinterklaas. You don't know Brian? Give him a Google, then you'll know what I'm on about. Mind you, Brian wouldn't be up a chimney would he? Probably down the pub having a pint of ale, like a man with sense. Unlike me, with no sense, stuck up a chimney and probably never going to get out and I might stop breathing soon and oh no oh no...

NUFF, GET DOWN THIS CHIMNEY NOW OR I'LL STICK YOU ON THE TIPPY-TOP OF MY TREE NEXT YEAR!

Calm down, Nicky, calm down. Panic will do you no good at all. Maybe if I twist my arm like this – whoa, at least that dislodged something. I think I can get my fingers to it, I... *ew*! It's all bony and feathery and, *ew*, gooey. I think it's... *ugh*, dead bird, probably, and I poked my fingers into it. Ick ick ick.

NUFF! WHAT THE HELL ARE YOU PLAYING AT UP THERE? BRING YOUR WAND DOWN HERE THIS INSTANT, YOUNG FAIRY!

Bumholes, got a mouthful of grit there. Tastes like burnt - wait, what was that? I'm sure I heard something. Yes, there it is again. Noises beneath my boots. Sort of a scraping and a tapping. Is someone down there?

"Yes, ma'am, it is early! Never mind, I'll soon have the fire roaring and then the children can come down!"

Uh-oh.

RED CHRISTMAS

Ruth Long's 'Bad Santa' flash fiction prompt invited writers to turn the Christmas spirit on its head. This is my take on that challenge.

The pale skin resisted for one tantalising moment before parting under his assault. He dug deeper, searching for the pulsing vein, and grunted his satisfaction as it was pierced. He sucked greedily, and the hot blood coursed down his throat, new and fresh. It flowed easily, spilling from his lips and staining his whiskers. Above the usual iron tang, he could taste cinnamon and sugar. She'd been eating scones.

At most houses, of course, he simply collected the blood. Even his huge belly could not hold the blood of every child in the world. So he stored it, up in the ship – sorry, *sleigh* – taking a few drops from a slit made under the tongue with his fingernail. The amount taken was not enough to be noticed from a single child. When multiplied by the number of children in the world, however, there was more than enough to sustain him through the year. He drugged them first, of course. It would not do for them to waken during the process. A handful of – well, let's call it *Fairy Dust* – ensured that there would be no sudden nightmares for the little darlings.

This child though, oh this child he had not been able to resist. Tired and peckish after a long time-slowed night, he had been slow to sprinkle the *Dust*. She had been awake when he had arrived, face flooded with delight as Santa appeared in her bedroom, her wide blue eyes twinkling with life and surprise, blonde tresses framing a face full of joy. Her expression hadn't slipped as he threw himself at her and ripped the nightdress down over her shoulders, exposing her vibrant skin. His teeth ripped at her neck before the beatific smile had left her face.

It never ceased to amaze him, the blithe acceptance by humans of his existence, of his immortality. Their assumption that he was benign and loving. Did they never question how he managed to return, year after year, century after century, never aging? That they fell constantly for the smoke and mirrors of the merry outfit and the cheap gifts spoke volumes for their blinkered idiocy.

A rattling gasp close by his ear told him that she was close to death. Swiftly he drew his nail across his wrist, loosing his own blood. He pushed the girl's mouth against it. Her lips moved only slightly, sliding weakly against the bloody skin. She was almost gone. He had left it too late.

No, wait. She stirred, and her tongue slipped between her lips. She lapped at his blood, then sucked harder to draw more out of him. She was feeling The Thirst. His timing had been exquisite. He twisted his fingers in her hair and tore her away from him. She snarled and tried to bite him. He grabbed a mince pie left out for him, dipped it in her blood and crammed it into her gore-streaked mouth.

"Now, little girl, come with Santa. You'll enjoy being an *ELF.* Ho ho ho!"

NATIVITY

Another story for 'Tales by the Tree'; this one is very English in feel. Miss Brightsmith is, as any number of you will know, named for one of my favourite authors, Alex Brightsmith. Go find her on Amazon.

Miss Brightsmith smiled happily. This year's nativity play was going extremely well, a stark contrast to last year's disaster. Everything that could go wrong did go wrong last year. The baby Jesus losing his head, which rolled into the front row of the audience. The innkeeper saying to Mary and Joseph "Yes, come in, there's plenty of room." Worst of all, the Archangel suddenly getting severe stage fright and weeing himself before sitting down in the puddle and bawling his eyes out.

This year, however, the children were doing her proud. Kara James was word perfect as Mary, and her brother Ethan's Joseph, though snotty, was performing with a bravado that made the audience of indulgent Mums and Dads chuckle.

This year Miss Brightsmith had, for once, decided to take a seat in the audience rather than standing fretting in the wings, and it was paying dividends. Much of the tension was lifted out here among the smiling, Christmas-spirited adults perched awkwardly on chairs that were just too small. Here she was able to appreciate the play for what it was; a joyful slice of Christmas fun presented by five-year-olds, rather than a professional production that had to be word-perfect.

"And lo a mighty star..." announced Lisa Shambrook, projecting her voice just as Miss Brightsmith had taught her. This was just perfect. As the youthful voices joined to sing '*Away in a Manger*', she looked about her. Most of the audience was beaming, eyes moist as their offspring sang to them the same song that they too had sung for their own parents decades ago.

Now that the play was nearing its end, several of the smallest children were becoming tired or bored. Shepherds fiddled with their trousers, stars waved to their mummies and sheep picked their noses. There only remained the crowning moment when the Archangel appears to bless everyone and to prompt the singing of the final carol. Following last year's disaster, Miss Brightsmith had decided to try something different this time. She had built a fairly high platform to the rear of the stage, unobtrusive until lit by a single spotlight. She had chosen the brightest boy in her class, the eager and enthusiastic Caleb Walker, as her Archangel. He had listened intently as she instructed him how to carefully climb the steps and step into the spotlight right on clue. She had impressed upon him the importance of his role, and he was determined to present the Archangel properly.

"Don't worry, Miss. I won't let you down," he had piped cheerily. "My Mam always says the show must go on."

"You should always listen to your Mam," she had smiled. "Be careful not to let go of the handrail when you're on the platform."

"I won't, Miss. I know the angel's important, and I know what to do. I'm not nervous or anything. The show must go on."

Caleb's moment had arrived. Right on cue, he appeared behind and above the assorted children on the stage. The audience gasped. The new arrangement had worked better than Miss Brightsmith could have dreamed. The Archangel seemed to materialise out of thin air, and he looked ethereal and translucent, glowing with light. His paper wings wafted gently, looking almost real. Caleb spoke his line with a meaning and conviction that belied his age.

"Joy to all here assembled! May everyone find true happiness and love through all their life. Harken to the heralds of peace!"

Everyone in the school hall joined in a rousing rendition of '*Hark The Herald Angels Sing*' as Caleb faded out of the spotlight and the hall lights came up. An enthusiastic round of applause filled the hall as the song ended. Afterwards, parents sought her out and congratulated her on the wonderful production.

"Miss Brightsmith?"

She turned round, beaming, ready to accept more praise, but her face adopted a puzzled expression when she saw that the man who had spoken was a serious-faced police constable, his hat gripped in his left hand.

"Yes?" she raised her eyebrows, "Can I help you?"

"It's about Caleb Walker, I'm afraid."

"Really? I can't imagine why you'd be interested in him. He's one of the good ones, never any trouble.. He'll be getting changed right now. I'll see if I can find him for you."

"I'm sorry," the constable laid a gentle hand on her arm. "Your Headmistress was supposed to have told you already, but apparently there was some sort of mix-up with the secretary not passing on a message. The Head only discovered that you hadn't heard a short time ago, when I arrived to make certain arrangements. Since I am trained in such matters, I offered to tell you the news myself."

"I don't understand."

"My apologies, I'll speak plainly. Caleb Walker was run down by a hit-and-run driver on his way to school this morning, and suffered massive head injuries. He was rushed to hospital, where the doctors did everything they could, but I am afraid he died from those injuries at about eight-thirty this morning."

"But—"

"I'm sorry that you weren't told. You must have been worried when he didn't turn up."

"I thought... I think he might have."

"Hmmm," the constable nodded, his expression a mix of confusion and concern, possibly for her state of mind. "I see that you managed to find a stand-in for your angel, anyway. The show must go on, eh?"

"Yes, yes. Bless him, Caleb was always determined that the show must go on."

A CHRISTMAS GIFT

A Christmas Gift *was my third piece for the marvellous (and hefty) Christmas anthology, 'Tales by the Tree'. This one is rather more serious in tone, but no less magical than the others. If you believe in that sort of thing.*

My Own Edith,

I don't know how properly to start this letter. The circumstances are different from any under which I ever wrote before. I won't post it for now but will keep it in my pocket. I write these words on Boxing Day. I never imagined, when this damned war began, that I would still be separated from my sweetheart at Christmas. I miss your voice, your smiling eyes.

We go over the top soon. If the worst happens perhaps someone will post this. If I survive, I will post it to you myself with kisses added. Lieutenant Reith should by rights censor our letters, but I'm told that he hasn't the heart for it, and I'm hopeful that it will one day reach you intact.

I have your latest letter here; a ray of light in a filthy world. I'm very glad to discover that you appreciate Cornish pasties. So do I, and often eat a hot one when on my way back from town. Can you fancy me climbing the hill, cane in one hand and a hot pasty in the other? Quite a study for one of your snapshots! I look forward to a lifetime finding out more things about you.

Thank you for the socks. They were most welcome. You cannot imagine how awful are the conditions here. The freezing trench is filled with mud, ordure to the knees, worse things that I cannot describe to a lady. One pair of socks kept my feet warm as intended, while the second served well as gloves as I stood watch on Christmas Eve.

I was on the firing step, trying to keep warm, listening to Ames' gramophone recording of *"Roses of Picardy"* playing repeatedly. When it ended for the hundredth time, I heard other music in the frosty air. I heard singing from the Hun lines: "*Stille Nacht*". Keeping low, I glanced over. There were lighted candles along the lip of the Hun trench, exceedingly pretty in the frosty night. As the carol ended a guttural cry went up.

"English soldier! English soldier! A merry Christmas!"

The Bosche were calling to us. I could not help myself, and answered.

"*Glücklich Weihnachten* to you too, Fritz!" I shouted, hoping my schoolboy German was correct.

"You sing now, Tommy!" one of them laughed, and sing we did. Through the night we exchanged songs, then came the dawn, pencilling the sky with grey and pink, heralding another day of pointless slaughter.

I peered over the wall, my hand gripping my rifle, and my eyes widened. Some ten feet above no-man's land hovered a strange glowing light, bright in the approaching dawn. It twinkled and shone. No flare this, for it hung motionless, a pure radiance. I reminded me of, well, a star.

You must understand, darling, what living with constant death and dismemberment does to a man. It makes him to fear nothing if he knows that at any moment he may be blown to smithereens. I laid down my rifle and set my foot on the wooden ladder.

"Private Fulton, do not respond!" hissed Lieutenant Reith, "It's a Bosche trick!"

I ignored Lieutenant Reith and clambered out of the trench. I stumbled over the rutted mud towards the beautiful light. As I reached it, it faded and disappeared and I looked down in disappointment. In a crater at my feet lay perhaps a dozen dead Germans. I then realised one of them was moving, and moaning softly.

"Tommy! Merry Christmas! We come to meet the brave man who greets us! We have wine! Will you share with us?" I looked up to see four Hun walking nervously towards me, arms out, carrying bottles. They were smiling broadly. Were these the savage, brutal barbarians that we had been told about?

"You have a wounded man here!" I beckoned to the approaching Saxons, "*Schnell! Schnell!*"

The Germans hurried to carry to safety their wounded comrade, one Otto Dix apparently. I do hope he survives. Soldiers from both sides wandered out to join us and we commenced to talk, to laugh. The Germans were not at all evil. They were very decent chaps.

We exchanged cigarettes, chocolate, wine and stories. I showed one man your photograph. He declared you '*zehr schöne*'. He showed me a picture of his three young children, all of them with dark curls and happy smiles. We looked forward to a time when we could embrace our loved ones again.

All Christmas Day we relaxed, conversing and singing together, comrades in an unofficial truce and united in hatred for this bloody war. We wrote our names and addresses on field service postcards, and exchanged them for Bosche ones. We cut buttons off our coats and took in exchange the Imperial Arms of Germany. But our gift of gifts was Christmas pudding. The sight of it made the Germans' eyes grow wide with hungry wonder, and at the first bite they were our friends for ever.

At eight, Lieutenant Reith fired three shots in the air, put up a flag with '*Merry Christmas*' on it, and climbed on the high parapet. The Bosche raised a sheet with '*Danke*', and the German Captain appeared also. These two bowed, saluted, then dropped into their respective trenches. The Hun fired two shots in the air, and the War was on again.

I don't think I will ever—

-

It is with real sorrow that I must add to this letter some very bad news about your fiancé, Private Michael Fulton. He played a very gallant part in the attack on the German position made by this regiment on 26th December, 1914. He helped his company commander to a place of safety after the former was wounded, but in doing so was hit by a shell fragment and died immediately. I cannot tell you how sorry I am. Everyone thought so much of him, and admired his fine sturdy character and unfailing cheerfulness.

He it was that led us to maintain the truce described above, and for the gift of peace he gave them on Christmas Day scores of men will be eternally grateful. Let pride then be mingled with your tears. May God comfort and console you.

Lt. John Reith, 8th King's Own Regt., BEF

ABOUT THE AUTHOR

A Yorkshireman living in the rural green hills of Lancashire, Michael Wombat is a man of huge beard. He has a penchant for good single-malts, inept football teams, big daft dogs and  the diary of Mr. Samuel Pepys. Abducted by pirates at the age of twelve he quickly rose to captain the feared privateer *'The Mrs. Nesbitt'* and terrorised the Skull Coast throughout his early twenties. Narrowly escaping the Revenue men by dressing as a burlesque dancer, he went on to work successively and successfully as a burlesque dancer, a forester, a busker, and a magic carpet salesman. The fact that he was once one of that forgotten company, the bus conductors, will immediately tell you that he is as old as the hills in which he lives. Nowadays he spends his time writing and pretending to take good photographs. Michael Wombat has published over one book (cubicscats.wordpress.com/buy/). Other authors are available.

> *Photography: Wombat's World (wombat37.wordpress.com)*
> *Twitter: @wombat37 (twitter.com/wombat37)*
> *Facebook: Page (www.facebook.com/wombatauthor)*

ALSO AVAILABLE

Moth Girl versus The Bats

A steampunk-inspired novellette with a flavour of old movie serials inspired by singer Thea Gilmore.

Out of the moonlight they sped in their thousands, swift as death, razor wings glittering in the pale glow of the Wolf Moon. In the frost-shrouded city below, the final toll of the curfew bell faded. Latecomers hurried inside, the hems of their capes whisked through narrowing gaps as doors were slammed, shutters bolted and chimneys blocked.

Those without homes huddled in hidden crevices, or burrowed under piles of rubbish as the bats hurtled out of the night sky. A high keening filled the air – whether emitted by the mechanical creatures themselves, or created by their sharp wings slicing the air no one knew – and suddenly the streets were filled with vicious whirling things, shredding anything soft that they happened across: clothing, flags, living flesh.

Where do the deadly mechanical bats come from, and what is their purpose? Can songstress Thea use them against their creator to prevent the people of her town being slaughtered?

Available in paperback, for Kindle, and as an Audiobook.

Cutthroats & Curses: an Anthology of Pirates

An anthology of pirate yarns edited by Michael Wombat, and including two linked Michael Wombat stories.

Be excited, you swabs, for the tales collected in this timber-shivering volume play fast and loose with their uniting theme of piracy, and will carry you on a heart-thumping voyage to far-off places beyond your salty imagination.

You will sail the seas of ribald adventure and discover a mighty treasure: a rousing collection of wind-powered, piratical short stories from eleven of the finest indie authors writing today. Join them on the high seas for a dozen swashbuckling tales that are not afraid to flirt with fantasy.

Featuring stories from Lisa Shambrook, Boyd Miles, Marissa Ames, Bryan Taylor, Beth Avery, Matt Jameson, Eric Martell, Michael Walker, Stephen Coltrane, Alex Brightsmith and Michael Wombat, this is a treasure that will reward everyone.

"The collection is capped, fore and aft, by the joyful irreverence of editor Michael Wombat's own Mr Crow"

Available for Kindle.

Soul of the Universe

An anthology of music-inspired stories edited by Michael Wombat, and including two of his stories.

"Music gives a soul to the universe, wings to the mind, flight to the imagination and life to everything." - Plato

Here you will find a collection of six stories by four authors that, at first glance, seem to have little in common. Here are Science Fiction Adventure, Medieval Fantasy, Emotional Drama, and Steampunk. You will even find a Western. Though each of these stories seems to have little in common with its companions, every one shares the same genesis. They were all inspired by that same divine spark that gives the universe purpose. They were all inspired by music. Each of the authors in this collection takes a favourite song as their muse and tells a story that no one else could hear. The result is an endlessly entertaining collection of well spun yarns, thrilling adventures, and emotionally engaging drama.

"This collection will captivate you, it will pervade your senses and it will absolutely enchant you."
"Each of these stories holds a special place in my heart."

Available for Kindle.

Warren Peace

A novel for older children and adults.

Influenced more by Seven Samurai, Zulu and Joss Whedon than by Watership Down, Warren Peace is about a young, nervous rabbit with an easy life – easy, that is, until the foxes come. With the lives of his friends and family in danger, Cuetip must undertake a perilous journey out into the big world to find help. On the way, he also finds terror, laughter, sadness, friendship, humans, cats, gods and perhaps most important of all, courage.

A novel about talking animals, but definitely not for tiny children, *"Warren Peace"* will grab both your heart and your funny bone and shake them silly.

"Beautifully written, intersting, funny, emotional, inspiring story."
"Could not put this quirky, humerous book down."
"The genuine article; a story that succeeds on its own merits."

Available in paperback, for Kindle, and on iTunes, B&N Nook and ePub.

Fog

Definitely not for children, this novel. Fog is an adult thriller.

You know how it is. We've all experienced it while driving. You suddenly realise that you have no idea where you are, or what your destination is. After a few seconds light dawns and you remember where you are going. But what if light didn't dawn? What if you continued to know nothing before that moment? You have no idea where you are, who you are, or why a bunch of nutters is trying to kill you. The only thing you know is that you have to run for your life...

Sexy, funny, violent and thrilling, Fog is not so much a Whodunnit as a Whatthehellsgoingon.

"Very clever. Funny and genuinely shocking at times."
"A joy to read. A rattling good yarn."
"A pretty damned amazing ride."

Available in paperback, for Kindle, and on iTunes, B&N Nook and ePub. Also available as a SPECIAL EDITION HARDBACK.

Cubic Scats

A gathering of rib-provoking and thought-tickling posts from the many blogs of Michael Wombat.

Featuring a skeuomorphic cover by thrusting young designer Thom White, this mighty book includes musings, Oliver Cromwell's head, fiction, a ghost chicken, odd facts, history, a bone-eating snot-flower worm, dreams and yes, recipes. Amazingly, Wombie has also managed to pack over 300 photographs into this little book (and reader, beware: in one he is as naked as if he had no clothes on at all). Why read all these remarkable articles for free on the internet when you can buy them all in this handy, easy-to-read-on-the-bog format? Buy this and save yourself hours of Googling.

"A perfect read for the beach. Or train journeys." - Alex Brightsmith, about another book.
"Don't drag me into this." - Dawne le Goode.
"Where did you put the bread knife?" - Mrs. Wombat.

Available in paperback only.

7731777R10077

Printed in Great Britain
by Amazon.co.uk, Ltd.,
Marston Gate.